THE COCKTAIL HOUR

Sophia Hillan

THE COCKTAIL HOUR

ARLEN
HOUSE

The Cocktail Hour

is published in 2018 by
ARLEN HOUSE
42 Grange Abbey Road
Baldoyle
Dublin 13
Ireland
Phone: 353 86 8360236
Email: arlenhouse@gmail.com
arlenhouse.blogspot.com

Distributed internationally by
SYRACUSE UNIVERSITY PRESS
621 Skytop Road, Suite 110
Syracuse, NY 13244–5290
Phone: 315–443–5534/Fax: 315–443–5545
Email: supress@syr.edu

978–1–85132–194–0, paperback

Typesetting by Arlen House

Front cover painting: 'Hazel in Rose and Gold' by Sir John Lavery

Back cover painting: 'Skycurve' by Gary Sloan (2012)
is reproduced courtesy of the artist

Printed and bound in the UK by ImprintDigital.com

LOTTERY FUNDED

CONTENTS

ACKNOWLEDGMENTS

'The Broom Tree House' was first published as 'A Surprise' in *Literary Miscellany*, ed. Sam Hanna Bell, *Ulster Tatler*, Belfast, 1979 and was a prizewinner in the 1979 BBC/*Ulster Tatler* competition judged by Sam Hanna Bell and Paul Muldoon.

'The Cliff Path' was first published in *New Irish Writing*, ed. David Marcus, *Irish Press*, October 1980. It was a prizewinner at the Open Short Story Competition run by Listowel Writers' Week, June 1980 and was shortlisted for a Hennessy Award in 1981.

"The Cocktail Hour' was first published in *The Faber Book of Best New Irish Short Stories*, ed. David Marcus (Faber & Faber, 2005). This story was shortlisted for the Royal Society of Literature's first V.S. Pritchett Memorial Award, 1999.

'Roses' was first broadcast on 3 July 2007 on BBC Radio 4 in the series *Defining Moments*, read by Michael J. Reynolds, produced by Heather Larmour.

'Portrait of Elizabeth' was commissioned by and first broadcast on 27 February 2015 on BBC Radio 4, in the series *Sitters' Stories*, read by Laura Carmichael, produced by Heather Larmour.

'Anna, by the River' was first published in *Literary Miscellany*, ed. Glenn Patterson, *Ulster Tatler*, 8, no 46 (August 2012).

'Under the Light' (extract) was first published in *Reading the Future: New Writing from Ireland*, ed. Alan Hayes (Arlen House/Hodges Figgis, 2018).

The generous assistance of the Arts Council of Northern Ireland in the publication of this book is gratefully acknowledged.

for Ronnie Buchanan,
who steered the craft

THE COCKTAIL HOUR

A PRINCETON MAN

'Watch out,' said Julia, 'he's coming over.' She turned away, beautiful shoulders hunched high, like the vulture she was. Close as a cloud of starlings, the others followed suit, shutting him out. No matter: he thought as little of them as they of him.

They would open up again when they saw who was with him; which they did, the tight flock wheeling round once more in his direction.

'Why, there you are,' crooned Julia, 'you *naughty* man! Where have you been hiding, this whole summer long?' He might have said, 'In plain view', but it was unnecessary and, as quickly emerged, redundant: the moment he introduced his companion they ignored him, plying the newcomer with questions about England, about that handsome King and his American divorcée – so thrilling! And, yes, oh yes, of course, his work, his recent and much-lauded work. No one had read it just yet, but they all planned to, very soon – and was it true that it was to be made into a picture? It was, confirmed the visitor from England, and his friend here was to be one of the writers on it.

How those pencilled eyebrows rose, how those cigars hung momentarily suspended, as the group turned from the Englishman to stare instead at him in all his sad-eyed insignificance. ('Really,' said Julia later, 'rather like the King, or the Duke, whatever he's called now – I wonder I never noticed – and both, you know, finished, completely finished.') They waited while he smiled, and shrugged and made the sound of modest deprecation; though everybody, including himself, knew he would not be one of the writers on the picture, if it ever did get made. On this third and, doubtless, last chance in the whole tawdry business, he knew he was here simply to put his daughter through school; and acceptance, even on sufferance, might take him through the length of the evening. He could have done with a drink; but he was not going to take a drink.

He stepped back a little: they liked to get their kill fresh as possible. Preparing to drift, he found to his surprise that one of the group had moved beside him. He couldn't quite place him, not that it mattered. The man was fairly new: a director, European and, like himself, not specially welcome in this company.

'Tell me,' said the director – what *was* his name – taking his elbow, and indicating with his head, 'Isn't that young Jimmy over there? With Spence?'

Before he could answer, the group turned as one to see the new attraction. You couldn't miss Spence: stocky, pugnacious but, it was agreed, somehow trustworthy. 'Sure,' said Julia's husband, 'long as you keep him off the sauce.' They clinked their glasses to that, until Julia's sidelong, warning glance in his own direction checked their merriment.

'Now, Jimmy,' she said, brightly, deliberately, 'I would rather like to meet.' She paused, running a carmined fingertip round the rim of her glass, and sighed a little: 'I do like a young man to be tall.'

All the men straightened up. The women murmured assent.

'And those eyelashes,' said one. 'He can bat *me* with those any day he likes!' There was a little silence. She was Julia's sister, from out of town. She wouldn't be asked again.

'Ginger says he's a better dancer than Fred,' volunteered the director, and they all turned to him in passing gratitude.

'Oh, Fred!' said Julia, leaning in toward the other women, her voice low and thrillingly conspiratorial. 'Ever try to dance with Freddie off the set? Watch out for your toes!'

There was a ripple of delighted laughter, and they all set to think of something else they had against Fred Astaire.

'Princeton man,' he said, then, first thing he had said for months that anyone listened to; and they stopped in surprise.

'Astaire?' said Julia's husband. 'No, you're wrong. Astaire's been on the boards since he was a kid.'

They laughed loudly then, their derision trained back on him once more: imagine not knowing that about Freddie. But everyone knew this sot had Princeton on the brain. Wasn't he supposed to have been a Princeton man himself? Or no, maybe that was Oxford; but anyway, it just went to show that you couldn't pay heed to anything he said, and in fact it was a mistake to encourage him. Then Julia, who knew perfectly well not only that he had been dry for months, but also that he was indeed a Princeton man, and that he was talking not about Astaire but about the handsome Jimmy, stepped forward and took him by the arm.

'I'll tell you what, darling,' she said, her voice a diamond. 'Why don't you go and bring him over here and introduce us? Jimmy, I mean, not Fred.'

More laughter.

'Yes, do,' said the director beside him, not unkindly; but well, to be suddenly in the set because of a lucky crack about Astaire, something like that couldn't be given up for, face it, a broken-down has-been like this fellow. All the same, even a has-been could be useful. 'Listen,' he said, voice carefully lowered, 'I've got this project, well, an idea, but it looks like it will be a project for sure if I can just get the right people.'

Silence.

'There's a part in it for a Princeton guy – you know, your kind of guy. You could maybe, you know, sound him out for me? And,' his eyes wary, the director looked about him, voice still carefully below the pitch of the group, 'maybe you could write on it? There'd be a credit in it for you. Guaranteed.' Then, raising his voice, he clapped his still silent listener on the shoulder. 'Sure,' he said, loudly, 'Julia's right – you go right on over there and get that boy!'

A credit. Guaranteed. If he had a dollar for all the times he ... but, before he could respond, the director too had turned away, and the group closed over once again, as if he had never been there; which, as he reminded himself setting out to walk towards the young man, was probably fairly close to the truth. As to sounding the boy out, the only thing he would sound him out about was Princeton, and how the old place was.

A Princeton man. What those words had once meant. When he was at Princeton the world was his, spread out before him for the taking. And he had taken it, and all that it seemed to offer; and now, here, in this inferno of bauble and illusion, he was compelled to pay. What circle of damnation he was in he no longer knew; what the painted and corrupt he passed had done to earn their place in hell was a matter of indifference. There was a blonded starlet, harlot, flinging herself at a man three times her age, in full and unblinking sight of the third wife daily humiliated by him. Here was an arrogant young stage actress, newly arrived from the East, angular and brash as a boy, crashing across his path without a word of apology, hotly pursued by a much-married, much-ridiculed former star of the silent screen. Beside him, surrounded by women, stood an ambassador's son, rake-thin, shock-haired and startlingly handsome, born to privilege and accustomed to indulgence; the kind of boy his daughter must never be allowed to meet. Everywhere he looked, the predatory and the hunted moved as in the dance, as at a Venetian carnival, a masked ball. And in the shadows of the periphery, avoiding the glinting, clinking glasses overflowing with the nectar he dare not taste, he exchanged once or twice with the older and the wiser a glance of jaded understanding of the ritual of ambition and betrayal. That brother and sister, for example, saluting him with their habitual courtesy: one confined to a wheelchair, the other statuesque, observing the pageant with that ironic detachment for which she had been famous on the stage and, latterly, the screen. What was that famous line of hers, from the play everyone remembered: something like, that's all there was, there wasn't any more. Was that what she was thinking, as she steered her brother's invalid carriage towards the door; signalling with her weary, still piercing eye the end of the painted glory that this place of mirrors and fantasy had always been?

And this boy he was going over to speak to, was he too to be broken in the game of grapple and flight that all these evenings inevitably became? Jimmy, they had called him. Jimmy, Jim and the more dignified James: he had heard him referred to by all of these; yet, whichever he was, just now he was standing quite alone. You could tell a fair amount about a man standing by himself at a party; but what he saw in this young man gave him pause. It was not just that he stood head and shoulders above the rest of them, for that was nature's doing. It was something else, something he recognised, a kind of careless elegance he hadn't seen since, oh, it must have been 1913, a winter day at Princeton: his first Romantic, a football star, so modest he wore his letter on the inside of his jersey, kicking with casual insouciance from behind the line. And this boy, this Jimmy, he had all that, and something else: a reluctant smile, a shy smile that illuminated his boy-scout's face until it was suddenly beautiful. It struck him forcibly, painfully; even as he reached to take the hand the young man so readily and gracefully extended at his approach.

'I think we may have something in common,' he said, his heart filling with an almost paternal tenderness. The young man's eyes, puzzled, perhaps wary, questioned him.

'Princeton,' he said, closing the boy's hand in a firm, friendly grip. 'I think we may both be alumni?'

He saw the young man's face clear, and felt his arm relax.

'Why, yes,' came the reply, gentle and eager. 'Class of '32!'

They exchanged names, and 'Jim,' he heard, but as luck would have it there was a burst of music as the band started up, and he heard himself shouting over it: '... anyway, I'm thinking I should change it and call myself something like, I don't know, John Darcy. I'd like to see if they'd still publish me – and I'd certainly be amused if my daughter read it and wrote me a fan letter.'

He saw the young man's smile of tentative appreciation. Then, 'what are you writing at the moment, Mr ... Darcy?' he heard. Had his name not registered at all?

'Oh, don't worry about the John Darcy business,' he said, fighting resentment. 'I mightn't even use it. As to writing, I'm working on a number of projects. I'm sure you know what that's like.'

Even as he spoke, he saw that the boy didn't yet know what that was like, and remembered, with a return to compassion, that this was a youngster, like his daughter, an innocent among the wolves.

'That's enough about me,' he said. 'Tell me about you and Princeton.'

'Why,' said the young man, and he ran his hand in perplexity through the shining tumble of his hair, 'I don't know that there's so much to tell. I got through, I suppose, but not much more. I'm,' he paused, and smiled again his slow, enchanting smile, 'I guess I'm not much of a scholar when you come right down to it. Can't spell, for a start.'

The cameras would adore him. Women would swoon over that boyish modesty.

'I wouldn't worry about that,' he said. 'I could never spell, and I never let it hold me back, at Princeton or anywhere else.'

'Well, sir,' said the boy, 'I suppose it didn't always matter, at that. Didn't hold me back in the Triangle Club, that's for sure. But my grades ...'

He stopped hearing him. The Triangle Club. Once, he himself was a shining light, no, *the* shining light of the Triangle Club. Wrote for it, acted in it – should have made President, until the war; until the summer he got a crazy urge to go and be part of something that had nothing to do with anything ...

'When was that, sir?' he heard and, though embarrassed at having spoken his thoughts aloud, was struck again by the gentleness, the vulnerability of the young voice, and thought: he will be destroyed. He thought of his daughter, and his heart as a father contracted.

'What would you be,' he said, 'What would you like to be if you weren't here?'

'Why, an actor, I guess,' said the boy, simply. 'Maybe on the stage. I mean, that's what I spent most of my time doing at Princeton. I did have thoughts of becoming an architect; would have pleased my father, and I might well have if ...'

Then, 'do it, son,' he heard his own voice say, with a firmness that surprised himself. In the same moment, not needing to look, he sensed, as a wounded creature might sense, the approach of the predators. They had wasted no time: the director must have said something that interested them, something to bring them over here and it could only be about this boy. They were circling, scenting new blood, and he entertained for a second the absurd notion that, if he had the inclination or the energy to look, he'd spy, abandoned somewhere in the room, the bones of the English novelist, picked clean.

'Jim,' he said then, earnestly, as he would to his daughter if, God forbid, she were here and in this danger, 'why do you want to waste your time and your good education on these ... on these ...' Words would not come. What words were there for what they did here?

The young man's face, gentle, diffident and at the same time, resolute, seemed suddenly a wrenching symbol of everything this place set out to destroy. Maybe he couldn't be saved, maybe he wouldn't need to be, and maybe – who could say – he wouldn't want to be.

'Listen, son,' he began, 'You've got to ...'

Then, 'yoo hoo!' he heard, and knew it was Julia, bearing down. People were turning to look.

'Yoo hoo! You've got to introduce us to this young man!'

What was he doing? He would lose this job, like all the others. Maybe just let him find his ... but in spite of himself, he took hold of the boy's arm and tried to draw him away.

'Go back,' he heard himself say. 'Just go back to Princeton. Be an architect. Don't stay here: they'll scoop you out. They'll take what you have and toss you to one side when they're done.'

The young man still smiled, but there was a certain resistance in his arm, and the smile, he saw, held in its kindness more of tolerance than comprehension or companionship.

'Don't you see, sir,' said the boy and, though he was playing to no audience, he could not have given a more sincere performance. 'Don't you see that I have to try? That I ...' he hesitated, charmingly, then straightened up, like a soldier, 'that I have to, well, make the effort? Isn't that what Princeton was about, if it was about anything?'

Yes, he could see him doing all that on screen, but, he was tempted to reply, what if you try, what if you try your best, and it makes no difference, no difference at all? But there was no time. They were closing in. One last effort then, for himself. He reached in his pocket.

'Here,' he said, handing the young man one of the few, the very few dog-eared cards he had left. 'If you like to telephone, that's where I'll be.'

He saw the boy open his mouth to thank him, but they were already upon him. They were clearly not going to wait to be introduced: the director looked all set to do that. There was just enough time to step back before they elbowed him out.

Good luck, son, he thought, and God knows you're going to need it; then, turning away, something at the corner of his eye made him look back. The boy was standing where he had left him, as if he hadn't seen Julia and her crowd, as if he were quite alone. He stood there, staring at the card, and then he looked up.

'Scott Fitzgerald,' he heard, in the boy's soft voice. 'That was Scott Fitzgerald.'

'Yes, well, you said it,' said another voice, damning and dogmatic: Julia's husband, naturally. 'That *was* Scott

Fitzgerald. Long time ago. Right now, son, that's nobody at all,' and the rest of them dutifully laughed.

They all laughed, except for the boy, who stood, unmoving, looking straight at him, candid as the morning sky, holding him in a blessed moment of recognition. Yet, even as he raised his own hand to salute him, he saw the young man, his sleeve summarily, proprietorially taken by Julia, turn to her, and adjust with admirable and possibly unpractised skill both his look and his smile. He dropped his saluting hand and turned away.

At the door, about to escape into the quiet of the summer night, he thought of staying to watch the dumb show that was surely about to unfold; of standing, a watcher on the lawn, like his long-ago narrator of the book that everyone once prided themselves on having read. Yet, why bother? He had tried, in the Princeton way, though it probably wouldn't make any difference. Instead, meeting the eyes of the old and dignified brother and sister who had once dominated the stage of New York, he exchanged with them in silence what all three of them knew, without rancour, to be true. That's all there was. There wasn't any more.

THE CLIFF PATH

They were all very tired now, but Mary kept on walking and walking. Catherine was dragging her feet, and John's hair was beginning to stand up in angry damp spikes. Gerard was just tired, tired all through, and he knew there was no point asking Mary to stop. He knew from experience that the length of the afternoon would depend on her mood.

It was still very hot, though nobody said. None of the children dared, and Mary had hardly spoken since they left the house. Gerard was beginning to feel uneasy too, because he knew from the direction they were taking that she might lead them to the cliff path. If he reminded her that they were not allowed, she might round on him and he shrank from that. Apart from anything she might go on it just to spite him; you never really knew with Mary. Perhaps she had forgotten they were not allowed to go there, because it was so dangerous. Perhaps she was just about to change her direction, and go towards the strand.

The thought warmed him. He longed suddenly for the gritty sand, the cold salty shock of the sea. He had been hoping when they set out that they would be brought there. John might build one of his dams and he could help Catherine make a sandcastle. Mary might sit in the sun till her ankles swelled, and then she would rush them all into the water in a sudden flurry.

While Gerard dreamed all this, it was already too late. She was going to the cliff path. He should have known she wouldn't bring them to the strand when her day was spoiled. Mary was very particular about her time off, and this should have been her half-day. She had told Gerard she would go into the next town and do some shopping. It baffled him that someone would want to spend any part of a precious summer holiday in shops when they could be on the strand, but Mary seemed to like it better than anything.

He had been in the kitchen when his father came in and asked Mary to take the children out for the afternoon. They did not realise Gerard had heard, or that he understood enough to know what was happening. At least he thought he knew. It would at least explain why they were not allowed to say goodbye to their mother before they set out. If he was right there would be a new baby, or else – and he tried not to think too much about this – maybe his mother was very ill, or dying.

There had been no time for questions. Mary had just hustled them out the door without towels or togs, without anything to eat, without letting them take even a sixpence from their moneyboxes. They all complained, but Mary said they would have no need of money, and anyway there was no time.

That was when Gerard knew it would be a bad day, that she would keep them walking until she had got over her disappointment. There would be no picnic, no trip to the shop to look at games or books, no sailing their yachts beside the dinghy pool. Certainly there would be no ice-cream at the Café Lido, and they'd been promised it if they stayed good yesterday, which they really had. Catherine would be difficult. She had just got over a summer cold and was still cross and babyish. She was complaining now in a very low whinge, but she knew better than to let Mary hear her. Mary was good if there was something really wrong, but it would have to be bad to get her attention when she was like this. There would have to be blood, or a temperature.

Gerard was feeling hot and ill-used, though he was not sure why. This confused him, and made him feel still more cross, but he couldn't show it because he was never out of sorts. That's what they said about him; *Gerard is never out of sorts*. Well, he was out of sorts now, but there was nothing to be done about it, though the effort of keeping it all inside was making his head ache, with colours in front of it. And as well, he felt really anxious, because if Mary said anything to him he might give her a smart answer, another thing he was famous for not doing, and anyway, he mostly liked Mary; but she was horrible today, and his mother might be dying while they were out here, perhaps because they were out here walking where they were not allowed, and if she was dying, they would be the last to know.

She should not have brought them here. He stared at her back as if he could force his resentment through her spine. He could hear nothing but the scuffling of their sandals on the small stones. They were all lagging behind now, and John was breathing hard through his nose, another bad sign. Catherine was snuffling, and Gerard took her hand out of compunction, because the sound was getting on his nerves. It was Mary's fault; he could hate her if he tried, if he kept on staring at her broad back, if she were not usually good to them, and a big help to his mother. That was what everybody said about her, she was a big help to his mother. Well, so was he, but he didn't boss everybody round because of it. He shook his head. He was not going to think about his mother until they were nearer home, because there was just too much to think of, and nobody to give any answers. He would concentrate on Mary's back, plump beneath her cotton dress, and help Catherine over the rocky bits.

He concentrated so hard that he missed the moment when they stepped on the path. It was not the big cliff path, the forbidden one, with great stones at its edge, high above the sea and the black, jagged rocks. It was another, a little tiny, creeping rabbit path, a green grassy path out of secret dreams of adventure. Excitement that was also apprehension washed through him. If the big broad path was forbidden, how much more would this one be, so narrow and unprotected? On the other hand, no one had actually forbidden this path, so it might be all right to go on it. Gerard pressed down the outraged voice protesting at such doubletalk and forced it to enjoy the heady freedom of forbidden pleasure. His head swam with the logic of it; Mary had taken the decision, and he had been on the path before he knew what he was doing, so it couldn't possibly be his fault. Mary was the adult, so she was meant to know what she was doing.

And then his confidence fell away, because he realised in one dreadful second that Mary did not know what she was doing. He felt it as she took his hand and told John to take Catherine's other one. He heard it in her voice when she told Catherine to stand in near the cliff face. Most of all he saw it in her feet, shaking slightly as they inched along the path. They were at a bend, and as they rounded it, Gerard saw why Mary was suddenly nervous. The path was so narrow that they would have to walk with their backs to the cliff face. He knew too, without her telling him, that she could not go back, that she could not take the responsibility of letting them go first. He gripped Mary's hand tightly, sorry, deeply sorry for having wanted to hate her. He couldn't begin to hate her now when she had done something so very wrong, and he even felt a kind of sympathy for her when she said brightly across him, 'nobody's to worry. This is a quick way, and it'll take us down to the sea in no time, and then you can play on the rocks. Won't that be good?' No-one answered.

Gerard was not fooled. He was glad he couldn't meet John's eyes because he suspected he was not fooled either. Catherine, however, seemed happy, humming to herself between their hands, and he tried to keep his left arm and hand relaxed and calm, in case she felt his panic the way he had felt Mary's.

A cold cloud obscured the sun, and a greyness swept over them. Catherine stopped humming and began to whimper. Gerard would have liked to give her hand a small encouraging tug, but she was just too far away for it to be safe. He was far away himself, somewhere up in the proper cliff path watching them, watching the fear grow cold inside the person who should have been him. And then the cold turned into drops of wetness and he went back into himself. That was rain, not spray, and Catherine was wailing, 'Ma-am-my! Ma-am-my!'

'Stop that noise, Catherine,' said Mary, too sharply. 'Don't be such a baby.'

Catherine dropped back to her whimper, but Gerard felt his earlier anger return. She had no right to speak to Catherine like that. All this was her fault. They were in danger; she had put them in danger. Gerard would have liked to do what he never did, to shout at her, to blame her for her bad temper. He felt rage starting low in his stomach, boiling up through him. It frightened him in short gasps; it might come out any minute, if Catherine did not stop whingeing that she wanted her Mammy, or if Mary said another word about the whingeing. He felt it getting out of control, rising in his throat. He couldn't stop it.

And then John stopped it for him. John, who had scarcely spoken since they left the house, spoke now. 'There's going to be a new baby. It might be there when we get back.' Gerard felt stunned, and a little put out. Why had John not said he knew? He was almost going to make it part of his anger, this new feeling that was so strange to him, when he realised there was no need. He felt in himself a lightness; for if John knew, part of the burden of worry was off him, and now the idea of his mother dying seemed silly, when John knew too. John would never allow an idea like that, so perhaps he needn't worry about it either any more.

Catherine was jiggling on the narrow ledge. 'A baby?' she cried. 'A boy or a girl baby? What colour of hair?'

'A girl,' said John, without hesitation. 'With dark hair.'

'It could be a boy,' said Gerard, light of heart, glad to be able to take his fear out into the open and let it go. 'Maybe a redhead!' He spoke without thinking, and felt too late the strong tug on his arms as Catherine began to yell. 'No a girl, a girl like me! Dark hair, like me, John said, like me!'

In dismay, Gerard realised too late what he had done, for already Catherine had pulled too hard. Her feet scrabbled on the loose rocks and for a horrible moment one brown sandal dangled over the dark roiling water. In silent terror, Gerard's eyes finally met John's; he knew in that instant he should not have spoken, that John was doing his best to keep her calm. He knew that the sandal over the sea could be all their bodies in another second.

Mary saved them. She kept steady. She nearly pulled Gerard's arm out of its socket, but she kept steady, and she kept telling John to do the same, to stay quiet and calm. And it worked, because then Catherine grew calm too, calm enough to stop flailing and regain her footing. It was really only one foot, and it had only just stepped on a loose bit of rock; in less than a minute they were all back to normal. Even the sea did not appear so menacing, but crept quietly beneath them as if it had not meant any harm, and they seemed to hear the seagulls for the first time in hours.

It was still raining, of course, but the air seemed quieter, as if the world had stopped for a moment while they caught their breath. It was not even so hard, once they got the trick of it, to shuffle sideways, and Gerard was not at all surprised to find that the path was, after all, leading gradually downwards. He should not have doubted Mary. The path probably was safe all along, if he had not been so ill-tempered and risked all their lives. That, he knew, would haunt him when everything else had passed over. He sighed, waiting for his next worry.

No one spoke as the path wound towards the sea, but this time it was from exhaustion. There was no resentment now in the air, and Gerard noted without surprise that by the time the path broadened and the big, safe road was nearby, John was walking quite companionably beside Mary. It left Gerard to cope with Catherine, heavy now with sleep, but that was all right. He deserved it.

If he had not been so stupid up on the cliff, he could be asking Mary now if she would use the telephone box on the road to ring up and find out about his mother. He might still risk it. If she said she would, he would know she had forgiven him; and then, as it happened, the same thought seemed to occur to her by itself, though Gerard did allow himself to think he willed it into her mind.

There was a long wait while she searched for the right change. There was another wait while she found the instructions on how to use the phone, and yet another while she read them. The two boys began to hop from one foot to the other, watching her lips move and her chin nod. After an age, she came out and, holding their breath, they tried to read her impassive face.

'Your mammy's feeling very well,' she said, looking kindly at Gerard. Inside him, a tightly-coiled anxiety unwound itself, like a sigh. 'She has a little sister for you all.' Her kind look became a beaming congratulation for John, and Gerard felt a pleasure that was almost painful at his brother's inspired guess. 'And she has dark hair, just like Catherine.' Mary, to Gerard's surprise, ruffled his sister's hair. She never did that. Catherine beamed sleepily, but she probably would have done that whatever was said, for she was almost unconscious on her feet.

It had somehow been decided that they would take the petrol bus home, though Gerard could not have said where or when. His eyes kept closing without his wanting them to. John had sunk to a kind of squat on the ground, his back against the telephone box, and Mary did not tell him to get up off the dirty pavement. The rain had stopped, but no one noticed. It seemed as if the green bus, its engine throbbing and trembling and its big black eye frowning at them, had arrived while they were not looking, and that Mary somehow got them on it without them having to do much about it.

They were all jumbled comfortably into one seat, the boys on either side of Mary, and Catherine on her knee, sound asleep. Gerard could just see John's hands, limp by his bare knees, and hear his regular, relaxed breathing. Mary was looking out the window, so close he could have counted the freckles on her nose. Waves of sleep tried to engulf him, but there was still one tight little knot of worry that he had to undo.

'Mary,' he whispered.

'Oh, hello there,' she said. 'You're back, are you?'

Gerard had no time for pleasantries. He had to get this straight.

'Mary,' he said, 'do we have to ... do you think we need to tell Mammy about ...'

His voice faltered. How could he put it without apportioning blame?

Once again, Mary saved him.

'Don't you worry about any of it,' she said. 'I'll tell her everything she needs to know; and I'll tell her, too, what good children you were.' She smiled. 'You just close your eyes now, there's a boy.'

And Gerard, absolved at last, passed peacefully into sleep on Mary's comfortable shoulder.

UNDER THE LIGHT

I don't know if I've mentioned before the effect of the street lamp outside our house. It is hard to explain, but it casts a curious light on all it touches. It lends to people and things a nostalgic air, softening outlines, making a kind of gentleness. I have often remarked its effect on my children as they come in from school on winter evenings. In an instant they become ethereal, ghost children, spirits of Christmas. Even my husband, when he is with them on their walks, or weighed down with books at the end of the day, seems a boy again, their brother rather than their father.

It was under the lamp that I saw, for the first time in many years, the woman who had been my girlhood friend. By its light, she became eighteen, nineteen perhaps – about the age she was when when my husband left her for me. I'm not proud of that, but it happened; and since I'm telling you this story you might as well know. Did I feel any unease, seeing her after so long a time? No; well, perhaps a faint twinge, nothing more.

Neither the illusion of youth nor that slight access of sentiment lasted more than a moment. Indeed, it was something of a relief to note, as she came down the path, that she looked her age every bit as much as I do – more perhaps, because she has let her hair show the grey. *Dunkelblond*, she used to be, in German class. *Cheveux blonds foncés*, in French. And I admit that it was nearly a source of satisfaction to me to notice a slight, arthritic limp as she walked. It meant that I could safely welcome her to my home. I might even find it in myself to pity her.

Yet, I forgot to pity her as she entered the hall and I saw her clearly. Avril. I was suddenly overcome with emotion at her presence, and was for a second, no more, almost inclined to tell her everything – of my mother's dementia, my father's protracted death, that time I – well, perhaps not that, but unaccountably, something about my life with David, who once thought he loved her. Yes, I had missed her. Before I knew where I was, I had thrown my arms about her neck and held her as my children used to do me, not wanting to let go. I could not see her face, the cool, familiar eyes, but I did not sense reluctance. I was, at last, nearly glad in my heart that David had asked her to come.

For, yes, I am ashamed to say that I had not really wanted this visit – except for residual curiosity to see what she had become, and to meet this husband of hers, the television man, American. He turned out to look quite remarkably like the young Jack Nicholson. You know, *Chinatown*. His name was Hubert – or it could even have been Humbert – but it hardly matters, because I immediately thought of him as Jack, and am nearly certain I called him so at least once. He was attractive, no doubt about that. She did all right. All the same, left to myself, and despite hearing about her stellar career from my one or two remaining school friends I would not have asked Avril to visit. It was David, of course, David, dazzled by her appearance at some charity function, David coming home full of it, of her, so pleased, so like himself again that I had not the heart to deny him what he wanted. In fact, it was I who found her, after he had virtually destroyed the telephone book by riffling so hopelessly through it. I said, 'David, there's the internet,' but he wasn't listening, so in the end I had to do it. He phoned though. I wasn't doing that; and, of course, they couldn't come on the first two dates he suggested – busy people, busy, busy – so I put a spoke in the next two they suggested. Those dates would have been perfectly all right; but, well. Anyway, they got something in the end, and I agreed, but – and I don't know why – once it was definite, the prospect sent me into a state, a panic like that time when I was so ill, but no, not at all like that, not really. I don't get excited about things anymore. Still, I cleaned and polished and did absurd, unlikely things, like sending the curtains – the curtains, for God's sake – to be dry cleaned. They shrank, of course. I cooked and I froze and I dived in and out of this cookery book and that cookery book, and changed the menu a dozen times, and rejected each change at three o'clock several mornings. Yes, well, the freezer is certainly stocked. We could survive a siege.

And then the evening itself arrived. Here she was, real, tangible, almost ordinary, in my house. I began to wonder what I had been nervous about. I had everything planned. We would have a drink, perhaps two, to ease any tension, and some light preliminary conversation, and then the meal, which could take up a leisurely hour and a half if I got the intervals right. I would keep the talk to general topics and if anything, anything came up about that old business, I would bring down our baby, our late bonus, as a – as whatever. I had made sure the bigger ones were taken care of, staying with their grandparents or their friends, but the baby stayed with us. I was torn, yes, between wanting Avril to see what David and I had, and not wanting to underline the fact that she and what's his name, Jack, have no children. I'm not cruel. Still I knew if I had to I would bring the baby down.

I thought it unlikely that I would have to. It is so long ago, and I am sure no one thinks of it any more. I don't. Yes, I lost some friends over it, but no one of any consequence. They said – everyone said, actually – that Avril was very ill over it. One person said there was a nervous breakdown. I don't know. I wasn't concerned with her problems that summer, with all that I had to cope with, not to mention keeping David together and fighting off the so-called friends who blamed me. She did get very thin, that's true. I thought it suited her. I mean, we were the Twiggy generation, after all; none of us ever minded being thin. And it's a thing that happens to girls in their late teens.

I wasn't callous. I did ask her about it one evening when, by chance, we were both coming out of the Old Library, not long after the start of Michaelmas term. It had begun to be cold and I could see, despite the maxi coat – I see they're back – and the long scarf that she was very thin and, I suppose, solitary. She had always been with David the year before, and I would have been alone, and joined them. Now he was waiting for me, and only me, in the Students' Union, and she was, what, going home on the bus by herself? Before I thought what to say, I heard myself speak to her, straight out, in our old way, 'have you been ill? They said you were ill over this.'

She looked at me without emotion. 'Over you and David Moore?' she said, without breaking her step. 'Hardly.'

And then she walked on without another word. That's when I called after her, 'you've got a great figure out of it, anyway,' but she didn't even turn. So you see, I did try; but I needn't tell you, I didn't try again after that. As for David, he told me she would pass him in the street, wouldn't speak to him at all.

So, as far as this dinner was concerned, I was determined if anything were to come up, it would only be about school, which is quite funny in a way, because that is where they taught us correct social behaviour for all occasions. Yet, when I thought of school – which I don't much because I hated it – forgotten things came back to me. I was there again for a split second, smelling the polish in the Assembly Hall, dancing in brown sandals one of those peculiar cavortings they made us do. I was always the girl, because I was small, and Avril, because of her height, the man. And the shocking thought came at me out of nowhere, as clear as it was untrue, that I had been without a friend all those years. The sensation was painful, and so intense that I could scarcely believe she was not similarly struck. I turned to say to her, 'Avril – the Gay Gordons! Do you remember? The *Schotissche*?' but I did not speak, for I caught her eyes upon me in that instant, their expression so guarded, so utterly detached from me, that I was momentarily halted, excluded from my own memory.

It chilled me, right through my body, as in a cemetery. Yet, the room was warm and welcoming as I had made it, and we sat down to the meal in what passed for harmony. I had taken such care, and now I could hardly remember what I had prepared. The feeling passed, however. After all, as I looked at her again, it occurred to me that I might have imagined that earlier hostility. She was calm, relaxed, even charming as I knew she could be. When we were at school she was quick and witty. It never seemed to matter what she said – it was her manner; part Katharine Hepburn, part Greta Garbo. Her quality was that she might, at any minute, say something wonderful or wildly comic, something that would start us off. Then, as quickly, she would withdraw and we would be left, and have to let her be. No one knew what she was thinking, and she was often distant. She did a good Bette Davis when she was in the humour, and a memorable Georgie Fame; I think that is what dazzled David. He loves jazz and he adores old movies. He was fascinated, enchanted by someone so remote who could turn in a moment into another person, almost anyone, and be that person for however long the notion took her. Yet, in the end, even he grew frustrated by the sudden withdrawals, the utter refusal to be engaged beyond the peripheral. I believe he hoped, with increasing despair, for more, for at least the promise of something not yet revealed. I watched him, at first with a detached sympathy and, then, increasingly, with a kind of distress, because I knew he was wasting his time. This was all anyone would get. I think he realised that. I think that is what happened; he saw, as I had done, that the distance was all there was.

I watched David fall out of love and, while I did not – I swear I did not – plan that he and I would come together, it somehow happened; and the irony of it all is that it happened through our attempts to understand the object of our mutual fascination. As for Avril, as I have said, I didn't see her much that summer, and I have already explained what happened when I tried to approach her in the autumn. I know that she started going out with someone else, which she would hardly have done if she had been really grieved, and she was immediately surrounded by an entirely new group of people. I defy anyone to say she suffered anything more than hurt pride. I think, and the dinner I am describing certainly confirmed it, that she is fundamentally cold. David discovered this, and turned to me, and fell in love with me, and we have been happy. We have always been very happy.

I wish, all the same, you could have seen her at our table, her sideways looks at Jack, one eyebrow raised, and her old habit of writing her name in imaginary cursive script on the tablecloth. Over and over she did it. I remember her at that in school, in classes she disliked. She still had that trick of laughing in a faintly derisory fashion, and I did not miss how David stopped as he heard her laugh, and glanced quickly at her, and drained his glass like water. I watched how she met her husband's sardonic eyes across the table, in perfect, silent understanding. I'm sorry no one could see me, poised with the coffee pot above her shining head – in which, by soft light, it was almost impossible to detect the white hairs – for I believe anyone would have admired my restraint as I poured with care and with grace into her cup, and handed it to her without touching her fingers.

David. David behaved like a complete fool after that. He spilled coffee over my last good tablecloth. He knocked it over, gesturing, telling Avril some stupid story, and it flew not only over the cloth but also over the newly-cleaned curtains. He was a clown. He was also drunk. He insisted that Avril sing, and she laughed him away, protesting. He insisted, his speech slurring, she refusing, his face nearer and nearer hers, those cool grey eyes suddenly shining, light-filled, until her foreign husband leaned in and said quietly to her – only I heard – 'better do it, sweetheart.' Did he say it in German, or did I imagine that? *Schatzi*? Did he say that? Then he turned to me, suave and seductive and he murmured, 'she has a remarkable voice, you know,' and I smiled, but only with my lips. As if I, of all people, needed to be told that, I who sang with her for years in the Choir, week after week, every Corpus Christi at the procession, and every Christmas in *Messiah*. Yet even I had forgotten her voice, its unexpected and startling range. Hopelessly, I saw that David was once again bewitched, as I had seen him all those years before; eyes for no one but her.

And now she was singing – I couldn't believe it – the old songs we learned at school, quaint songs we laughed at in those days, all shepherdesses and storms, young love and lost love, and before I could stop myself I was singing with her, until that moment when our shoulders touched. It was

41

just a moment, a touch, a split second in spontaneous harmony; and I felt my heart soar with delight, with sheer joy that she had come back to me. Then she stopped. She stopped, and time stopped, and while I still knew there were others in the room, they were dimmed somehow, because all at once it was the long ago and we were again in the Assembly Hall. A president was being buried in Washington, and with all the world we grieved. Outside in the grounds, the November evening closed round our darkening windows, trees stripped of leaves under a heavy sky, but far away in Washington the heavens were blue, the air clear as morning for a speeding soul. I knew in that second's memory that it was all right again with Avril, that none of what happened in between really mattered, because friendship endures, and I folded her arm through mine and I said, 'the day Kennedy was buried – do you remember I said to you, "all the hope's gone out of the world"?' And she turned full to me, blank-eyed, a cold Medusa, and she removed her arm.

So broke the spell. Of course she remembered. I got up, as though to make more coffee, and Jack took the hint. He rose to his feet, helping her from the low cushions – the imprint of my head and hers still upon them – saying they must go, was that really the time. David, sober and attentive – how did I think he was drunk – was already standing. As we moved in silence to the door, Avril was beside me. I handed her into her soft coat, and held out her silken scarf but, this time, made no move to embrace her. She, however, extended to me a graceful hand, in a formal, impersonal gesture. Taking it in the same spirit, I wondered how I had failed to notice the very slight beginnings of gnarling, of twisting at the knuckles, the already misshapen thumb. It occurred to me, without emotion, that she would be crippled some day.

We made the usual noises about returning the visit, promising to phone, to write, not to lose touch, but I think I will not see her again and I think David will not either.

I did not go to the gate. I stood in the doorway, waving into the night. David walked down the path with Avril, and behind them, at a little distance, strolled Jack. Their car, sleek and dark, waited just beyond our streetlamp. David paused to wait with Avril for her husband. As I watched they turned in the lamplight to face each other. Suddenly, they were framed, a young couple in kindly light while I, an old crone in the darkened doorway, watched him take both her hands and for one, long moment, hold them in his own. I closed my eyes. When I opened them, they were standing some little way apart and her husband had joined them. Formal farewells were being made, a final joke, men's voices in private collusion. Avril's husband helped her into the car; the engine throbbed in the night; an arc of white light swept out, rendering pale and insubstantial the lamp outside our house; and then they were gone.

David, alone and seeming, in the newly-softened lamplight, vulnerable and young, looked after them for a time, while I grew cold and damp in the black porch. I do not know how long he would have stood there, had it not happened that our youngest called out his father's name. David, startled, seemed to shake himself like a sleeper awakened and, turning up the path with his usual walk, passed me on his way to the child with the briefest of smiles, and the pressure of his hand upon my arm.

I watched him take the stairs two at a time, calling reassurance to our Benjamin. Nothing was changed. In the end, nothing had happened.

ROSES

They stood at the door until the car had disappeared. Last to go was the young man's bravura salute, the dazzle of the blonde girl's smile. Until they were out of sight he kept his hand raised. She held her own smile. He touched her elbow, a gentle pressure, and the smile was put away. In the cool darkness of indoors, they stopped to reassemble their day.

He stood for a moment, wondering again what the thing was he had been trying all day to recall. If he was patient, it would come. He moved a cushion which had been disturbed by the young people. Normally, Marian would see to such things; perhaps she was tired, like him. There was a blonde hair curled brightly against the deep red of the cushion. It touched him, quickly, just for a moment. He said, 'nice girl,' then, 'nice couple.'

'Yes,' said Marian, taking the cushion from him.

'Didn't you like them? Didn't you think she was pretty?'

'I liked them well enough,' said Marian. 'She was pretty, yes.'

'I thought she was a nice girl,' he said, puzzled. She reminded him of someone. Who? He shook his head.

'Well, she's your type. I know who she reminds you of.'

He remembered.

'You're my type, Marian.'

She laughed, that sharp laugh that came from her lately.

'Don't be earnest with me, George,' she said. 'Save it for the cameras.'

He drew a deep breath.

'He's a bright young man. Didn't you think?'

'Yes,' she said, threading away from the red of the cushion the single golden hair. 'He's bright enough. Bright enough to come here and flatter you into telling too much.'

She thumped the red cushion, hard, and tossed it down on the sofa.

'Well,' he said, and in spite of himself, he felt an old stubborn anger. 'Well, Marian,' he said, 'I wasn't the one who told him about Billy.'

'Why not,' she shot back, her eyes snapping. 'He's in rehab, isn't he? It's a *Success Story*; your little *wunderkind* said so not half an hour ago. And Billy's alive, isn't he? Not like ...'

She could hardly, anymore, say the name of their younger son. They did not know where his body was. There was no trace.

'Teddy died a hero, Marian,' he said. His voice was gentle, his hand raised to reach for her.

She lifted her head, her proud head, and he dropped his hand. She said, 'Billy lives a hero.'

He bowed his own head. When there was nothing to say, it was best to say nothing. He had built a career on doing just that. Truth, he had learned, lies in the silences. Again, he reached out his hand, and this time he touched her, brushing lightly against her bent shoulder. Then, leaving her in her own silence, he went slowly out to the garden. In the shade, in a cool tub, he had placed that morning a new rose bush, bought on impulse, a delicate pale pink and white. It made him think of Marian's skin when he met her first. He would give her the first bud from it when it flowered. Then she might forgive him for having grown repetitive and forgetful. Ah, what was it he had forgotten today? The rose bush almost brought it to him. Something hovered at the edge of his memory, like the shadow of a bird at the window. Just as he was reaching for it, coaxing it to stay, it flew away and his mind was again an empty space. He sighed all through himself, shaking his head. Then, stooping slowly, he teased out the roots of the bush, spreading them in the dark water, encouraging them to relax, willing them to help him remember. Still, darkly floating, inscrutable, they held their secret.

Memory held sharp thorns. That girl. He struggled to recall. He just about remembered the man he was all those years ago, his confidence gone. It took her, Marian, to bring him back. She, she did it. She told him what hope he gave to her, how he made darkness bright. She said; doesn't that mean something to you? He said to her; it means everything to me.

What did she just say in there? That Billy lives a hero? It was Teddy who died, Teddy blown to pieces somewhere far away. She didn't want Teddy to go, but the boy, he wanted to go, and George said: in our family we have always fought for the things we believe in. Teddy went. Then he died.

Was that it? Was that why she spoke to him like that today? Was it because of Teddy? It couldn't be. It couldn't be because of Billy. It wasn't Billy's fault he lived and Teddy died. All right, he got hooked on those ... but was that worse than waiting or not waiting for six o'clock to open the bottle?

Perhaps it was some small thing he had forgotten? Sometimes it was a small thing. Was he supposed to pick something up that morning? Maybe he was. Marian could make their guests laugh till the tears ran down, stories about George and the things he did when he got distracted. 'George doesn't have a memory,' she used to say. 'He has a forgettery.' And he would say, 'but I have Marian.'

The evening sun sat low in the sky. The dog, who had slept the afternoon away, padded across to him.

'You're getting fat, Boy,' he said to the dog, who flapped his feathered tail and leaned his head against George's knee. 'We should take a walk.' The dog thumped his tail once, politely, without enthusiasm. To spare them both, he said, 'Let's go see Mom first. See if she wants to come,' and the dog, panting as if he had been on a long, heart-pounding run, followed at his heels.

She was sitting where he had left her. His heart lifted inside him. Once, it had turned somersaults. Now, it lifted, quietly, like a wave on the shore. She was sitting there, her arms round the red cushion, holding it close. The dog climbed on the sofa, and she reached absently for him, stroking his bony head.

'Marian,' said George.

She looked up as though a stranger had spoken.

'Marian. Was it about Teddy?'

'What?' she said. She was distant, as if he had disturbed her.

'Did I forget something today about Teddy? I can't remember, Marian. You have to help me. You have to tell me what I forgot.'

Her face softened. She was his Marian again. He sat down beside her. She did not turn to him.

'It wasn't about Teddy,' she said.

'What, then?' he asked, willing her to look at him, recognise him. 'What? Not that girl?'

He hung his head.

She laughed, softly, without joy.

'No,' she said. 'That young girl is nothing but ... a ... a gnat bite on a summer evening.' She laughed again, more strongly, more like herself. 'She is like her, though.'

He could not think. His mind fogged.

'Like ...?' It cleared. It hurt. 'You mean ...'

'Yes. She is like her.'

'Oh, Marian, I ... What can I say?'

He dropped his head into his hands.

All that foolishness; how could that come up when he felt so old, so tired? He needed her. He loved her. Her. Marian. Not that long ago, long-dead blonde, a passion of one season, one ... picture. That's all it was. One picture.

'Say nothing,' Marian's voice replied, outside him. 'It's what you do best.'

He said nothing. The silence gathered. Gently, Marian put down the cushion, smoothing it out, placing it to the other side of her.

'Did you know,' she said, almost brightly, 'that I nearly caught you?'

He was dumb. She took his hand in both of hers. He could feel the small bones.

'You remember I came to visit you on set?'

He said, 'you mean ...?'

She said, 'yes, that time.'

'We met for lunch in the canteen,' he said, his voice low, trying to put it together.

'Yes. We did. But we nearly met earlier. When I came to your trailer. I brought you flowers. Roses.'

She squeezed his hand.

'We've always liked roses best, haven't we, George? I stopped outside, to knock, in case you were busy.'

Silence. He looked at her, his heart slowly tearing.

'And I heard you. Yes. I heard you, George. So, I threw the roses in the trash and went away, and later I fixed my face, and met you, and then I just sat her out. I sat her out, George. Did you know that?'

He shook his head. He could not see her through the hot tears in his eyes, yet he felt the warmth of her hands on his, pressing him, making him know.

'And I gave you Teddy, my Teddy, the following year.'

She took her hands away. He was alone. The world was falling in round him, crushing him. He said her name, but there was no sound. He looked at the ground. He could not look at her. In front of him lay the dog, head on paws, staring at something under the chair. He followed the dog's eyes. He could just discern a small red light, flashing. It should not be there. He should see to it. Transfixed by the red light, addressing it, he tried again to speak. He said, 'Marian. I am human. It was ... human error. I have never loved anyone but you.'

She replied to the air above him. She said, 'I know that, George. That is the sole reason I stayed with you, didn't take Billy and leave you to it.' She breathed in sharply, as if in pain.

He took his eyes away from the fascination of the light and turned to face her.

'Marian,' he said. 'Tell me what it is I have forgotten. I beg of you.'

She looked at him sideways with a trace of her old compassion, humour washed away, but still, still there, his own Marian. 'You ask me what you forgot today. You say you are only human.'

He waited, as in church, head bowed, hands folded. After some moments, between deep breaths, as if to breathe were difficult, she spoke again.

'Human,' she said. 'Of the earth. You are human, George. But ...'

Silence dropped again. Neither moved, until Marian spoke again, 'but, so am I. Soon,' and she touched her eyes with her hand, 'I will be even more human than you. And I'll see my boy.'

'Is Billy coming home, Marian?'

She shook her head.

'Are we planning a trip? Do you want to find where Teddy ...? It's far, but we can ... is that it? Is that what you want?'

She sighed.

'I am planning a trip, George, but you're not coming.'

Fog descended.

'Marian, I don't ... what do you ... ?'

She slid gracefully to her knees, turning at last to him, taking his face in her hands.

'Oh George. George. Can't you understand? '

She undid the high collar of her shirt. On her neck were markings, like arrows.

'The hospital, George. That was what you were supposed to do today. You were to pick me up from the hospital. You forgot. You came home here with a rose bush. You didn't wonder how I got home before you. It was me you forgot. Me. And I have something to tell you, George, and I can't make it easy.'

He was years away. He was hearing her tell him that he would soon be a father. He looked at her now, at the deep darkness of her eyes, at her hair, gold shot with grey.

'The tests are positive, George.'

That was it. Those were the words she used to say, with the babies; the tests are positive.

'Do you hear me, George? They're positive. The tests are positive. They cannot help me.'

There was a sound in his head like a buzzsaw. She gripped his face harder, so hard it almost hurt.

'I am dying, George.'

He looked past her. The red light was still flashing. The dog, pushing between them, sensing distress, licked her face, licked his, flapped his tail, panted. She sighed, and put her head on the dog's head, sinking into the sofa.

'Down,' she said to the dog, her voice weary.

George got up, then folded himself down to the floor with great slowness, the dog nuzzling beside him under the chair.

'They forgot their machine,' he said.

She said, 'what?'

'Their recording machine. They forgot it.'

'Careless,' she said.

'It's still running,' he said.

She gave a short laugh, her new toneless laugh without mirth.

'Well, what a story they've got, now,' she said, 'if you give it to them.'

He looked up. 'If I give it to them?'

'There will be only you.'

He turned back to the chair. The dog was trying to catch the red light with his paw.

'Leave,' he said to the dog, and pushed him aside. He pulled the plug out, hard. The light died. He took the small machine, carefully, from under the chair, as if it were a living thing.

'Marian, do you think they ... do you suppose they left it under there on purpose?'

'Maybe,' said Marian, almost in her old voice, almost again ironically curious at the ways of the world. 'I wonder if they are that smart.'

He said nothing. He uncurled, slowly, from the floor. Then he walked with slow deliberation through the door into the garden. The dog followed. George stopped suddenly at the rose bush in its tub, and the dog, right behind him, bumped with a grunt into his legs. George reached down to him, sliding his hand across the dog's greying head. 'Sorry, Boy,' he said. 'I'm sorry.' Then, he tucked the small machine under his arm, reached down with his other hand and took out the dripping rose bush.

'Let's go plant this for Mom,' he said. As he stood up, the little machine slid out from under his arm and, with a quiet splash, fell into the water. The dog heard it, and cocked an eyebrow, but George, shaking out the roots of the rose, did not see or hear. He had forgotten the machine, and the young people who brought it. He was going to plant roses for Marian, and bring them to her when they bloomed.

ANNA, BY THE RIVER

Anna lay in the long grass, blocking out the sun with one sandalled foot. She was listening to the river, and thinking of her father. Thinking was a blissful thing. A rabbit hole made her Alice; a glimpse of a hedgehog meant a little house under a hill where there might be a laundress, an excellent clear-starcher, to give her back all the lost pocket handkerchiefs of the world.

Before her father had gone, this was their place. He loved to walk and she, taking sometimes three strides for one of his, had been happy to be beside him on the towpath. The last time they had walked here she had almost managed to meet him stride for stride. Now Anna was nearly sure she would be able to match his step.

When she was little he lifted her up to see the trees nudging each other, whispering their gossip, shaking with surprise at what they heard. He would hoist her right up on his shoulders. Anna rode high above the world, jogging and swaying as if he were a camel, or an elephant, his jacket collar reins or soft ears. She could smell rain on his hair and the other, woody smell that meant him. On winter days she would see his breath spin out, a thin ghost. Up on her perch everything was clear. In the spring she had seen small fish silvering in the water, heard urgent melodies of unseen birds. He knew what they meant, who belonged to them. He told her their names and their stories. Sometimes his own deep song would resonate from his body through hers, spiralling warm up to her head, filling her with the fear of the troll, *fol-de-ol*, or the joy of the runaway train as she blew, or sometimes strange, sweet languages from other lands. She did not understand the words but she knew the story of the melodies, low and gentle or sad and sorry, and she learned to sing with him the sounds she heard. Her favourite song, running from him through her, understood through every bone and every nerve, was the song of a river. She thought it was this river, their own river. Now, as she lay in the grass by herself, she tried to remember the deep and patient words, to hear them in her head; he didn't pick cotton, he didn't ... Anna, moving the sun back and forward with her foot, could not remember. She thought, when he comes, I'll ask him the words.

There was a splash and a sudden ripple on the brown water. Anna sat up straight and alert, shaking flattened grass and seeds out of her hair. On the far bank of the river she could make out a shape, sleek and brown. The water rat? She liked to think that this was the riverbank – the River Bank, where Moley and Ratty met one spring morning. Anna no longer quite believed she would one day see the Rat and the Mole in their little boat, the picnic basket at their feet, yet it gave her a rush of joy to see what might be a water rat on their river. For an instant she almost thought her father was standing there behind her, just out of sight, pointing far out, far away, above her head, to the bend of the river where Toad Hall might lie. Now to turn, extremely fast, in a bright second, could mean she would see her father. So, not turning brought it closer.

Anna sighed out her hope, and stretched long legs before her in the grass. How strange a foot looked at the end of a leg. She hugged her knees tightly, glad of them in the cooling grass, tickling herself with the fine hairs on the bone of her knee. There were in the world so many stories. She could read them, but she did not want to, anymore. He was all the people and, sometimes, lately, when she tried to read those stories, she heard his voice so clearly in her head that she had to stop. So, she did not read them anymore. Yet, she thought of them, and of him, all the time. She would be working in school, or helping in the kitchen, or running in the yard to catch a ball and, suddenly, for no reason, she would think, Daddy, and everything would be grey.

Here, it was better. Here, by the river, thinking did not hurt. Anna rested on her knees, going in her head to winter evenings, safe and warm in her bed. He would tell her stories which she rarely heard to the end. He invented endless tasks for Cinderella, lowering his voice, adding more things, more lists, his voice dropping quietly in her head till Anna felt sleep moving across her even before Cinderella could leave the kitchen. She would hear her own voice, far away, saying, 'please get her to the ball,' but even as she said it, she would be slipping down a soft slope. Through her closing eyes she could see, coming and going before her, his face at once grave and merry, the lamplight catching the gold clasp of his glasses. 'I don't know if she'll make it tonight,' he would say, shaking his head. 'There's a great deal to be done, all that scrubbing and chopping, all that fetching and carrying and ...'. Perhaps she had always wandered away from his voice, sliding down and down into sleep.

Once, he brought her to *Peter Pan*. She sat, rapt, at the front of the theatre, living the story. She tensed and tried to stand, though still sitting, at the moment when Tinkerbell, failing to warn Peter that his medicine was poisoned, drank it herself in desperation. Peter, wonderful boy, rushed to the front of the stage, every child in his outstretched hands. Tinkerbell would die, he cried, unless they believed in fairies! Did they, he asked, did they? Anna, pulling from under her father's arm, arching her back and hurling herself upright, stood as tall as she could and cried, 'I do! I believe in fairies!' and the other children followed her. Tinkerbell was saved. Anna knew then that it could be so. People would come back if someone believed hard enough.

She had written about it today, in school. They had been told to make a story about a happy time. Anna had slid straight back into that time and, strangely excited as she smoothed out the new clean page, she took up her pen. While she was writing, lost and happy, Anna glanced up and saw, from a distance, a tall, grey man come into the room. Far away in another time, she was still looking up at a stage, in a warm darkness, safe within her father's arm, comforted by soft tweed as she nestled into his shoulder. And then, abruptly, a cold shadow fell over her, and a hand that she did not know reached past her, and took up her work.

Anna felt rage wash through her. He just lifted it up and took it, her private world, written only for herself and her teacher to read. She scrolled up her fists, nails digging into the palms with a pain that was almost satisfying. The man spoke to her. He asked her, his voice not unkind, when the visit to the theatre had been. Anna did not answer, staring instead at the blank wooden desk where the magic had been. Then her teacher, her kind teacher, was beside her, and the book was gently replaced, and Anna heard her say, 'Inspector, I should explain ...' and 'yes, let me see, oh, three months, perhaps four ...' and then Anna heard muffled word sounds, making no sense, flow back over their closed heads as they walked to the top of the classroom.

She fought to hold back the anger and misery breaking inside her. She practised her new game, being a good and quiet child. It was necessary in the playground. Sometimes it was necessary at home. Once there, she told her mother she was going out to play, threw down her schoolbag and ran to the towpath. Through her running breath she heard her mother's voice, and she paused. 'Anna!' she heard again and, when she turned back just once, she saw her mother's lonely face and heard the usual words, 'six. No later.' Then Anna turned and ran to the river.

And here, by the river, she had stayed. Rocking back and forth, 'they think he is gone,' she said to her knees, pulling the grass around them. 'They think he will not come back. But I know. I believe,' she said, 'I believe.' She waited in a silence that was full of the lazy buzzing of insects and the high songs of summer birds, waiting for the calm which she knew must come from him. And as it came, slowly, warmly, she talked to him.

'When you come back,' she said, 'we will go again to the office. I will work your computer if you are not busy, and I will sit quiet if you are. I will sit still and look at all the books in the tall case. I will count the files with your name on them. I will read your certificates on the wall. When they bring you tea, maybe you will give me your biscuit, even if you do not stop writing or counting. I will write stories for you to read later and I will draw for you. But, if you want, I will do nothing. I will just sit there. Only I will not, not, not let you out of my sight. I will stay with you always. I will stand outside your room when the light goes off and I will wait till you sleep. If you do not sleep, I will not sleep. And, in the morning you will still be there, reaching for your glasses on the chair by your side of the bed. Your side of the bed will be full of you. It will be warm and crumpled, not flat, not silent. It will be full of you. Then,' Anna said, 'you will not go away.'

All the coloured spirals behind her eyes moved upward and outward into the sun as she lifted her head from her knees. She looked around her, at the late summer day slowing down to evening. Shadows fell across her feet, and the church bell over the river began to strike six. It was time she was home.

Anna sped, long-legged, brown head bobbing, back along the towpath. She kept her eyes on the bright shutters of her house, and counted the strokes of the bell. As she reached the grey gable, she stopped once, for a second only. She looked across the river at the tall church spire, under whose lengthening shadow, in the fourth month of his death, her father slept.

THE DEPTHS OF THE SEA

Sylvie, of course, was French. She was born here in this walled city, this former fortress where inquisitors had tortured submission from frantic or fanatic believers. She knew this sandstone wall, the battlement he sat on, thinking of her; she had told him about the little town within the town after you cross the wide, still river on the narrow bridge, after you pause in the cannon spaces and lean over the thick walls, after you climb on cobbles that hurt your feet through your shoes (though maybe not those shoes, she said, not those show-off, rich boy shoes). She told him to come to this summer school to bring up his grades. She just didn't tell him that she wouldn't be there, not until he was about to go.

'You can still stay with my family,' she said, with that shrug that entranced him. 'My brother has a little house outside the *cité*, but,' and she did that thing with her lip that turned his heart over, 'not in the new town, of course. No one would live there.' Why, he asked. *Immigrants*, she said. He didn't get it, but it didn't matter.

'I'm sorry, Adam,' she said, and she did it again, that little *moue*, that little pushing forward of the lips.

'But Sylvie,' he said, helpless.

She said, 'I can't go. I have to work. My family is not rich.' In his head he heard, not like yours. So here he was. There she was. And no, all those techy tricks he knew better than anyone, all those short cuts with phones and computers and little bits of kit no bigger than your thumb, they didn't help. But sometimes – well, one time, when he first arrived – she wrote him a card. He kept it, her spiky, precise handwriting, the New York postmark that made his eyes fill up.

Adam pulled himself away from the battlement and the cannon, and the sandstone shimmering in the heat. He threaded his way downhill through gaudy troubadours and damsels and dukes and knights; tourists in shorts, children in heated distress, flat-footed, red-faced gapers in sandals and socks. He turned away from young couples in love, their happiness twisting in him.

At the bottom of the hill there was some shade; it was a little cooler, but heavy with the burden of the town's bins, sour with stale beer and the remains of something rank, maybe cabbage. Over the decay stood the door of a disused church, iron-studded, haughty; across its porch sat a grill, like an elevator gate in a late-night movie. He passed the two bakeries; one newly shut, *fermé* forever, though its window still promised fresh *baguettes* every morning and its proud nameplate said that it had been in business since 1890; the other, smart and glassy, survived, selling pizzas and fast things you could eat on the run. Adam liked the new one better in any case; the old people in the other bakery spoke French all the time even to themselves, and nobody was going to make him speak it if he didn't have to.

He shouldn't have thought about French; he remembered and burned with shame. Why did he have to go and say that stuff? Why was it his job to put the old guy – ok, the professor – right about Burne-Jones? But it said it

up there, up there on the wall; it said he'd stood before
that picture by the Dutch guy (Dyck, Eyck?) of the man
and his wife, all mirrors and windows, and old Burne-
Jones made up his mind he was going to do something –
look, it said it – as deep and rich as that, and it said he'd
never done it and now the time had gone by. It said it right
there. And Adam liked Burne-Jones. He liked the one
about the depths of the sea, where the mermaid is holding
on to the man under the water; she's caught him, and
that's it for her. It said beside it; *'Elle ne sait pas que l'homme
est déjà mort.'* She doesn't know he's already dead, that
she's drowned him, or he's drowned before she got him.
Maybe she doesn't care. Either way it didn't matter. It was
like the time when he was a kid they took him to that place
with the Impressionists and he saw the water move. His
dad said he couldn't have, but he knew he saw it move,
and his mom believed him. 'I know you can, honey,' she
said. This water was moving too, but that wasn't it, that
wasn't it; it was the music. He could hear it. The music of
the sea. He heard it; he could write about that if he had to
write some dumb paper, he could write about that, he
could make it sing, in French or anything they wanted; but
it wouldn't matter now, because the professor hated him
and he would fail him, and his last chance would be gone
and he'd have to go home and do whatever they wanted
him to do, and this time his mom wouldn't be able to do
anything to help him. He could have kicked himself.
Instead he kicked at and missed a stray cat leaping,
yellow-eyed and vicious, from a raided bin, hissing its rage
at him.

He turned the corner into his street; or rather, Sylvie's
brother's street, called after some big hero, Resistance
maybe, but war, anyway. Sylvie's brother's house stood
deep in a terrace of identical, brown-pale houses, their
shutters bleached and peeling. It was a quiet street, all the
houses warily watching all the others, except in the early

morning when the street-sweeper – the what, the *balayeur*? – rumbled and swished through the streets, marking its territory, spraying its pointless water over the soilings of dogs, waking the lazy not yet risen to go to market. He liked the *balayeur*, the sound of its name, the sound of it, the rhythm of it as he lay in the quiet of his bed, the light of the new day filtering through the shutters. Later, this time of day, very little happened in the street. Like its occupants, it dozed. Adam was meant to work then, to study, to complete his daily assignments. His room was at the top of the house, quiet, restful; a view of the castle, a living picture, a *riche heure* of a France that anybody would have given much to see; he had a table under clear light, no interruptions, no reason to do anything but the thing he was there to do. He had everything he needed, and he dreaded it, his steps dragging as he neared the doorway, reading once again, slowly, as if he had never seen it before, the dates and the heroic deeds of the street's eponymous hero, dead in the defence of France against somebody.

He did not, at first, see the figure below the blue plaque. He did hear a sound, and ignored it, but it came again. '*M'sieu*,' it said. He winced, hearing himself putting the professor right about Burne-Jones; hearing the old guy correct him back, '*Monsieur le professeur, s'il vous plaît.*'

Again it came. '*M'sieu. S'il vous plaît?*' At the corner of his vision he saw a dirty hand outstretched, raw as if it had been scraped, meaty and scrawny at the same time. It was held out in supplication and, immediately, for no reason, he thought of the professor's well-kept hand, turned over in elegant dismissal, the life line or the heart line interrupted. This man's hand, dark-seamed, showed no heart or life lines; it was more like a river on a map, spreading out like that river in India. Adam started to walk away.

'*Ah, M'sieu,*' he heard again. '*Une cigarette. Je vous en prie.*'

Despite himself, Adam turned. The eyes. The man's eyes were large, the pupils dark, unfocussed, wildly bright as if he had a fever.

'*Ça,*' he said, pointing at the almost-finished stub Adam held between finger and thumb. '*Ça,*' he said again, '*ce que vous avez finie.*'

Adam looked at it, practically done, and back at the man. Then, with a shrug, and a last drag at it, he tossed it on the ground to the man's side. He saw how his hands, and his knees, drawn up close to his body, shivered, even in such heat. He saw his worn winter fleece and his jeans grey with grime; his shoeless feet.

'Have it,' he said, as he stepped away.

The man made no move to thank him, reaching beyond him as if he were already forgotten, seizing the stub like a man starving. Adam was almost past him when he felt the sudden pressure on his leg. Startled, he looked down. The man's hand was round his ankle, hard, unyielding, like the slate-grey eyes that still, unblinking, stared up at him

'Hey!' said Adam, in a voice he did not know. 'Get off,' and he tried to shake the hand away.

'*De l'eau,*' said the man, signalling to the bottle in Adam's back pocket, his voice, low and harsh, as if rusty from lack of use. '*Je vous en prie.*'

Adam, nervously aware that he could not actually kick the man away, took out the bottle, warm now, two-thirds empty.

'Take it,' he said, his voice still stupidly high, a kid's voice. 'Be my guest.'

His breathing was still unsteady, and stayed so, even when he felt the hand relax, sliding over the expensive shoes with something like a caress. Freed, it was all he could do not to run. Angry at the man, ashamed of his anger and ashamed of himself, he turned back at the door of the house to see if he was still there, or maybe to make sure that he was not behind him. He was just where he had been, not looking anywhere near him; curled up, rolled up, like an infant, both hands round the plastic bottle, his head and neck vulnerable and exposed. Adam, pausing for one irresolute, uncomfortable second, turned the key and stepped quickly inside.

In cool darkness he let the thudding of his heart subside and, legs trembling, slowly mounted the stairs. Maybe he was coming down with something; but if so – and his spirits lifted – he wouldn't be able to go to class, and he sure as hell wouldn't be able to do any work. He was almost calm as he called out hello to Sylvie's sister-in-law. She didn't reply, but that was nothing new; he could see her at a half-open window, standing to one side of the rectangle of light.

'You saw him,' she said, in her throaty French way. How did they do that, French women?

'That guy?' Adam said, carelessly, easing down his backpack, hoping she had not seen his fear out there on the street. 'Sure. I saw him.'

He moved to go through to his room.

'You shouldn't talk to him,' said Sylvie's sister-in-law.

Adam stopped.

'Why not?'

She shrugged. She did that thing with her mouth, that thing Sylvie did, but he didn't like it on her sister-in-law.

'Because he's homeless?' Adam said; then, proud of himself, '*Un refugié?*'

Sylvie's sister-in-law looked at him as if he was an idiot. 'He's not homeless,' she said, and did that thing with her mouth again.

'He looked pretty homeless to me,' said Adam.

Sylvie's sister-in-law gestured with her head to the window opposite, pushing her hand into her lower back.

'There is his family,' she said.

Adam looked. A washing line hung from that window, coloured things that looked like rags, embarrassing rags, maybe underthings, flapping away like bunting. It was the only shameful window in the whole, closed street. He looked away.

'I've never really seen that before,' he said.

'They are *immigrants*,' said Sylvie's sister-in-law, and his heart in that second turned over: Sylvie, oh, Sylvie.

'Scum,' she said then. He stared at her.

'Watch now. Look. Every day at this time.'

With reluctance, Adam looked, carefully not seeing the underthings. A woman, little more than a girl, with hair so dark it was nearly blue, her arms, unadorned, shining gold, leaned out of the window with a basket, and lowered it down on a rope, slowly playing it out. (*Rear Window*, flashed Adam's head, great movie). He looked to see the contents of the basket. There was bread, he saw, and a piece of what might have been cheese. In an instant the man, no longer supine, no longer still and waiting, was under the window, pulling out the food and tearing at it with hands and teeth. Something flashed in the sun, and Adam saw him catch with one hand a bottle, like his own plastic bottle. Good catch, he thought; then, 'bastard took mine,' he said. Sylvie's sister-in-law, arms folded, said nothing.

The basket was hoisted back up, and the woman, with one brief look of – something, triumph maybe; maybe contempt – stared straight across at them. Something in Adam suddenly, painfully, settled. The basket was swallowed up in the darkness of the window and the woman as quickly disappeared, pulling the shutter closed. All that remained was the line of washing.

'Why doesn't she just let him in?'

Sylvie's sister-in-law shrugged, and his heart again pulled at him.

'He murdered someone,' she said. 'They say he cut him up in pieces.'

She sighed, stretched backward like a cat, and moved with slow deliberation to a chair. Easing into it, she picked up some knitting, small and white and soft, setting it on the mound of her lap. Adam, numbed, stayed at the window. His legs had begun to shake again. He could hear his own heart, noisy in the stillness.

'My God,' he said. 'Are you serious?'

There was no reply. She was counting stitches.

'Murdered someone,' he said, 'and cut them up? My God.' It really was *Rear Window*. 'Why isn't he locked up?'

'He was,' said Sylvie's sister-in-law, eventually, stifling a yawn. 'Now he's out. But his family, they don't want him. Why would they?'

'But they give him food? They leave him on the street but they give him food?'

'She does,' said Sylvie's sister-in-law.

Adam thought again of the dark, beautiful girl.

'Who is she? His sister? His wife?'

'His brother's wife.'

'So where's the brother?'

She looked at him once more as if he was very stupid. He thought again, with hot shame, of the professor.

'It was his brother he killed.' She paused. 'Because of her. *Une affaire de coeur. Crime passionel. Tu comprends, petit?*'

Adam, watching the man back sitting hopeless at his station, no longer looking up at the blank shutters, the heat of the day burning down upon his unprotected head, understood enough.

'I get it,' he said, that earlier coldness settling about his heart. 'She has him. She doesn't want him any more, but she has him.'

Sylvie's sister-in-law sighed. 'Perhaps', she said. 'They are scum, but it's not a new story.'

Adam, still looking across at the blank and shuttered window, his thoughts no longer tumbling about, felt his mind clear, like the air, like the sky after a storm.

'*Elle ne sait pas que l'homme est déjà mort.*'

'*Très bien, petit lapin,*' cried Sylvie's sister-in-law, suddenly animated. 'You are thinking *en français*! Your professor will be pleased.' She was just putting down her knitting as Adam, turning at last from the window, saw her lift up an envelope from the table beside her chair.

'*Alors*, I almost forgot,' she said. 'There is a letter for you – from New York.'

Now he could move; God, could he. He practically sprang across the room, the man and his murder forgotten, everything forgotten, and he tore the letter open, reading it and shaking, devouring it as if he too were parched and starving.

He read it, and read it again. Then he stood quite still, and remained so for some minutes; until, folding it with slow care, he found himself walking unsteadily to the door of his room.

'I'm going to lie down for a while,' he said.

'As you wish,' said Sylvie's sister-in-law, without looking up. 'Shall I call you for dinner?'

'No,' said Adam. 'I'm not hungry. Just maybe call them at the college. Tell them I quit, will you?' He turned to go into his room; then, abruptly, stopped, took off his shoes and held them up to her.

'Say, do you have a basket or something I can put these in? And maybe some kind of rope thing?'

PORTRAIT OF ELIZABETH

I shall have Cassandra, but I will not have Jane. That she should presume, a parson's daughter, with no connections but those we bestow upon her, upon all of them! Mama said I must avoid such distressing thoughts; I must calm myself, think only of my dearest babe, and my other sweet darlings. 'I am quite calm, Mama,' said I. 'You know I think only of my family's wellbeing.' I have made up my mind. Cassandra, being here, and mindful of her station, may remain. But Jane! That she should have dared! I had no inkling; I did not tell Mama, yet in truth, until this day, I had none.

I should have guessed. The spinster's cap does not deceive me. Does Jane Austen imagine that I do not observe that smile that is no smile, the watchful judgement in her expression? Why, to appropriate to herself my eldest girl while the others stand excluded!

'What do you write to my Aunt Cassandra, Aunt Jane?' asks my daughter.

'Why, that Kent is the only place for happiness,' Jane replies. 'Everybody is rich here!' My daughter laughs, foolish child. 'Ah, Fanny, you are almost another sister,' says Jane.

Indeed not. Through birth and advantage, Fanny will always be Jane Austen's superior. In time, Fanny will understand that.

Those Austens – yes, my darling, Sackree will take you now, Sackree, take the infant, my head aches – the Austens are after all very little above the common lot. There is a vulgarity there that no amount of acquaintance with good society may hope to remedy. I have tried. No one can impute to me a failure in duty to – I had thought to say family, but might with more accuracy say – dependants. Ah, I would that my husband were returned! I shall tell him what his sister has done, what she is! Oh, but my head, my stomach ... I must indeed calm myself, for the sake of the child.

There. I am calm. I am almost again the Elizabeth of that portrait upon the wall. I was scarce seventeen when I sat for it. Seventeen, more than half my lifetime ago, and so happily in love!

'Mr Austen,' I told Mama, 'is of a different cast to that of his natural family.'

'They seem worthy folk enough,' said she, though she did not meet my gaze as she spoke.

'You misunderstand me, ma'am,' I replied. 'He has been quite removed from their society; he can never resemble them in the least particular.'

'Mr Austen is a pleasant young man,' said my mother, 'and his proposals are satisfactory. I like him well enough.'

And so the match was made, the likeness taken. Aye, and I see no likeness of Miss Jane Austen on any walls in any house. So must it be when one is a dependant. She may content herself with Cassandra's well-intentioned sketches, but to sit for her portrait? I think not. Ah, but my portrait! Weary though I be this day, mother to eleven young souls, I have comfort in that image. I shall be remembered so, with birth, beauty and all the accomplishments a young lady may possess; and soon Fanny will be as I was. I must ensure that she make a prudent choice; that she not succumb to the pernicious influence of the unaccomplished Miss Jane. Why she ... but I will not think of her. She makes my pulse to race, and I will not have my pulse race: I must shake off this tiresome cold. I will think only of my family, of my dear husband, though he be not by my side.

'Such a day for shooting, my love,' said he, as he left this morning.

'Quite so, my dear,' said I. I might have said, 'you are indeed fortunate that you can rise, go out, do as you will; it would be pleasant for me to walk out on such a day, were I able to do so.'

I restrained the impulse. Indeed, I am all restraint. Yet, this heat, this burning; I must have a degree of fever.

'Everybody has the Godmersham cold,' I heard Jane Austen remark; no doubt she was diverted by our discomfort. She catches no cold, with her coarse brown skin and her stout boots. Those pattens that she and her sister wear in the lanes! Perhaps it is with my brother that my husband shoots. My brother! I cannot yet credit it; it cannot have been so, and yet Mama asserts that it is.

How my head aches. I have such twistings in my stomach, such feverish heat. I would that my husband would return, else I shall have to send for assistance. The Godmersham cold! I will not have that set down for scorn in her secret writings. What does she mean by this endless scribbling, these pages so hastily put aside as one enters? Of what is she so ashamed that it must be hidden? Why, my little May, scarce seven, recounts with delight how, all unseen, she witnessed Aunt Jane leap up from her mending, clap her hands with glee and run – run! – to the table and begin to write at speed, laughing all the while. I declare, I doubt her very sanity. And, what can she describe that is of any moment? What has she seen of the world, she, little more than a lily of the field?

No, there is no question. My husband must be spoken to. There must be no more talk of the Austens being to live nearby. When I want Cassandra, as now, I can have her; has not my husband, time and again, made the journey to convey her here? Beyond that, no more need be done; they have many places to go, many other relatives upon whom to impose themselves. I hear what Jane says, that she and Cassandra are just the kind of people to be treated about among their relations, for they cannot be supposed to be very rich. Ah, but then, to affect to be surprised, to be demeaned by the lesser rate so kindly offered by our hairdresser? Does she not wear her poverty like a banner? Are we to blame that her parents were less than provident? Or that her brother, my husband, had the good sense, when but a child, to recommend himself to Mr and Mrs Knight? That, in adopting him, they bestowed advantages which she has herself so recently enjoyed, at our expense? Does she imagine that we, constrained by the expense of two estates, fifteen farms and the duty of provision for eleven children, are possessed of untold wealth? I defy her to find fault with the modesty of our arrangements for, indeed, we live simply and practise many economies. We rarely go to town, even for the season; and have but one nursemaid, though six of the children are not yet of an age to be sent to school. She will find little to mock in our arrangements. Truly, my husband must soon accede to Mrs Knight's request and change our family name; he must place distance between us and the Austens.

How, how can Jane imagine herself to be our equal, to presume ...? I trace it back, yes, yes, it goes back to her ill-treatment of Mr Bigg-Wither, when old Mr Austen removed his family from Steventon. In her twenty-sixth year, unmarried and quite unblessed with either looks or dowry, she might have counted herself fortunate that any sensible man would make an offer. Yet, Mr Bigg-Wither did so; she accepted his addresses, under his roof, in the home he shared with his sisters, her particular friends. Then, next morning to withdraw her solemn word, and flee the house like an errant housemaid! Such arrogance to refuse an offer from a respectable man. My husband forgave it much too readily; shock, he thought, the loss of her childhood home. Yet, what parson's daughter does not know that the living must be surrendered when the parson can no longer perform his duties? What parson's family has any entitlement to property?

My husband began then to speak of making accommodation available.

'What accommodation can you mean, my love,' said I. 'Are we not always willing, within reason, to make our home open to them?'

I saw that no more need be done. I pitied Cassandra, indeed; in her youth, on the brink of a suitable marriage, she lost her future husband to fever. Yet, as was proper, she accepted her condition and adjusted her expectations. She does not set bad example, unlike Jane who, now I recall, even before Mr Bigg-Wither, made a spectacle of herself with young Mr Lefroy. His people did well to remove him. And, indeed, since then, has not rumour associated her with others? Weymouth, I have heard; and Lyme Regis. In my experience, rumour generally has some degree of foundation in fact.

No one can say I have not tried my best. When I consider the events of the summer three years since! I was indeed a little sorry for her, reminding myself that her father was but lately dead. I made no objection to her entertainments for the children.

'But what shall Mama's part be?' asked Fanny.

'Why, the Bathing Woman,' replied Jane, with her secret smile.

I consented. I knew what I was about. I set myself to watch what might be taught to my children. I had seen in Fanny's diary that she and her cousin Anna had been reading romances in the Gothic seat. I do not care to have my daughters reading romances, in the Gothic seat or elsewhere, and certainly not with a cousin already, by too much proximity, under the spell of Jane Austen. I taxed Fanny with it.

'But Mama,' said she, 'Anna says that we shall write a romance of our own and Aunt Jane will read it!'

'And I say, Fanny,' I replied, 'that I have better things for you to do.'

I made arrangements. I suggested that Jane change places with Cassandra at Goodnestone. Though I was disinclined to accede to my husband's persistent notion that a cottage might be found for them nearby, I might, had Jane proved more amenable, have entertained the thought of having them somewhere on our property at Chawton. I do not care for Chawton; its principal attraction would have been its distance from Kent. Observing her behaviour, however, I judged the scheme a bad one.

'They have brothers and friends enough,' said I, 'and there is generally room in every family for women who will make themselves useful.'

Upon my honour, I did not know when I spoke that she was present, so silent was she about her mending. I believe she heard me, for she exclaimed, saying she had pricked her finger upon her needle. Her face flushed red; she left the room. Almost pitying her, I sent her to my family at Goodnestone. Through my mistaken kindness, she took her mischief there.

All might yet have resolved itself, had it not been for my brother's unexpected arrival this summer, while she was yet with us, bringing about their first meeting in three years. Still, I did not guess. How well I was deceived when

Jane, dissembling minx, told us with saddened features – having dined with my brother the very evening before! – that she must leave directly, for she shortly expected a visit from Mr Bigg-Wither's sisters, her old friends, so long unseen; and with downcast eyes and lowered tones, reminded us that she could not disappoint them, for the personal reason that we knew, concerning her refusal of their brother. Ah, my trusting heart! Did I not encourage her, indisposed as I was, to remain with us until September? Yet, she would go; knowing she could be of use to me, hearing the children's reading, assisting with mending and sewing – for, at those, I will allow, her skill is beyond the common.

In good faith, we accepted her sudden decision and let her go. We did not guess that her sly reference to Mr Bigg-Wither concealed a darker truth. It was Mama, Mama, not half an hour since who, all unwitting, told of it.

'Ah,' she said, 'It did not surprise me that she left so hurriedly. I wondered that she would remain, with Edward so near.'

'My brother Edward?' said I. 'Why, he courts Miss Foote, does he not?'

'He courts her now,' she said, 'but I believe he would not have done so, if Jane Austen had consented to accept him.'

She needed say no more. I asked her to leave me, to let me rest, but I can find no rest. I know Jane. I know, as if I had seen it happen, how she must have set about engaging my brother's affections three years ago, as she did with Mr Lefroy and Mr Bigg-Wither; how she must this very summer have ensnared him into a proposal, only to have the pleasure of refusing him; she, a nobody from nowhere to humiliate a Bridges of Goodnestone! This, then, is her revenge upon me over the business of the cottage; my many kindnesses rewarded with ingratitude and contempt.

She believes her deception undetected. She thinks, for I have heard Fanny say it this very day, that she will soon be invited again, to drink French wine, she says, to eat ices, to be above vulgar economy ... Oh, but she will not ... That she might tempt and refuse him again, or even, dear God, torture us afresh by accepting him without love or esteem? That she might one day be Lady Bridges of Goodnestone Park, while I remain Mrs Austen! My temperature rises; I feel it; how my heart races; my stomach twists beyond endurance. Sackree! Sackree! Send for my ... send for help! Call someone, anyone! I will ... yes, bring her, I will have Cassandra ... *I will not have Jane ...*

The Broom Tree House

That Saturday, then, as soon as the others had gone, he set to work. He was so nervous that it was difficult to think, but he had to think. He had to get it all done before they came back.

Mary asked him what he was planning to do while they were away, and he told her he was just going up to the garden. That was true, but it was not all the truth. Mary always wanted to know what they were going to do, and sometimes she would be all right, but other times she would go straight and tell their mother. He hadn't told John either, because John would have had other ideas. Anyway, John might have told Mary, and between them they could have spoiled the surprise. And this surprise was going to be his.

Mary, running water into the sink, started to sing: a good sign. He crept as quietly as he could to the cupboard under the stairs, opening the door slowly, so that it would creak as little as possible. Leaning into the dark slanty recess, fearful all of a sudden that someone might have cleared the bag away, he could hear his heart jumping in his ears. Relief passed through him as he felt its comforting bulk. A moment later, like a silent accomplice, it was in the hall with him.

He had put everything together, bit by bit; and last of all he had managed to commandeer a small square cardboard box. This, too, lay waiting under the stairs, and his last anxiety eased as he reached in to feel the reassurance of its sharp corners. It was a good box. There was not even writing or a single advertisement on it to spoil it.

Light now, and full of excitement, he took the bag, placed it in the box and started through the kitchen with what he hoped was a casual walk. He was Gary Cooper: a man of few words, a man with a job to do. It did take quite a long time to be him the whole length of the kitchen, and the smell of herbs and a simmering stock – dinner! – distracted every sense. But he made himself go slowly, kept his mind clear, and it worked, because Mary did not turn round, or even stop singing.

Hefting the things through the backyard was not easy. He had to be careful not to knock the box against the wall of the coal stack; black stains would have ruined everything. He managed, however, and soon he was up the steps and in the garden, settling himself in a quiet corner behind the blackcurrant bushes, to the side of the broom tree. This was his tree. He had planted it from a slip his granny gave him, and he had watched it grow and start to bloom, like a golden miracle. But he would never bring its blossom into the house; that was unlucky. His granny had told him. It was not unlucky out here, and the scent was delicious; he could nearly taste it. He could hear it in his ears like the buzzing of the unseen bees, like the birds above who kept his secrets. And the broom kept him safe to get on with his work. Even if the worst happened, and Mary came out to hang clothes, he could still hide everything behind the broom as soon as she appeared at the bottom of the steps. He could be busy doing something by the time she came. He could be looking for a ball, or watching the birds, anything. It wasn't likely, though, that she'd come out when she had so much to do for later. In any case she hated the sun, because of the freckles.

Now that he was settled, he knew exactly what he had to do. First, using a very fine pencil and his school ruler, he marked out all the little squares on the sides, front and back of the box. He marked out the rectangles too, near the bottom at the front and the back. He wondered if the side would be better. He looked at it, and thought, but decided on the back; it should be the back, to be right.

Then, reaching in the bag, he brought out the most important piece of equipment, the Stanley knife. It had been his grandfather's, and it was dangerous. His granny had allowed him it only after he promised to be very careful; but he was careful. He knew he was. He even knew that he was sometimes too careful.

So, slowly, perspiration forming on his face, heat sitting on his skin, he cut round the pencil lines, leaving in the frame of the squares so that they could open out in the middle, like windows. He cut out two sides of the oblongs and folded them so that they would hinge back. Then he cut two sides of the front of the box so that he could open it out. It was hard to do it neatly, the way he wanted it but, in the end, though it took a bit of time, he was satisfied.

Sitting back on his heels for a moment's rest, he was hit by a new idea. It would mean using the paints he had for his Airfix kit, and that paint was hard to find. He needed it for his aeroplane. Still, paint would make all the difference. It was difficult to make a decision like that, one he hadn't planned for. Thinking, and without thinking, he reached up to the bush beside him and pulled down a bunch of not quite ripe blackcurrants: their sharpness brought him back with a start to his task, and he saw with dismay how high in the sky the sun already was.

Quickly, he started to work again, emptying all the matchboxes from the bag. He had a great many, collected over months. The night before he had taken them all upstairs and covered them with plain paper and paste, to save time, but he would have to go much more quickly now, much more quickly, or he still wouldn't finish in time. His breathing started to come too fast, but he knew what to do now when that happened. He slowed it down. He wouldn't run out of air; it was all right, he could breathe. He would be what his teacher had said about him on his last report; he would be *meticulous*. He would glue eight matchboxes together in L-shapes, really carefully, and he would wait for them to dry before he took the next step. To make himself go slowly enough he spelled out the word his teacher had used, *meticulous*. It sounded metallic. It sounded particular. It clicked and then rolled smoothly into place. Then he spelled it backwards, *suolucitem*: now it was a new word, mysterious and spiritual, like a prayer. When that was done, he judged the glue must be set, and he stuck the other boxes on the sides of the L-shapes. He sat back again on his heels. He had four armchairs. These he lifted gingerly, carefully, and placed them under the blackcurrant bush, right beside a red-coloured spider. 'Mind them,' he said to the spider. The leaves made a pattern on the chairs; he wished he had colours like that.

Next he took out from the bag the brown paper and the foam rubber. To get the foam rubber, he had had to promise John rides on his bicycle whenever he wanted them, and the front seat in the car every time it was his turn for three weeks. That was hard, but it was what he had to do. They were good, the foam rubber colours; red and yellow and orange, rainbow colours.

Whistling a little under his breath, he spread the stiff brown paper on the cement of the path, and measured it precisely, to fit the bottom of the box. Next, with his pencil and the compass he had, so luckily, just learned to use, he drew a complicated pattern of circles and crescents and triangles on the paper. He was afraid he might tear it, but he was lucky again and it didn't tear. Once he was satisfied with the design, he started to cut the foam rubber with the Stanley knife, keeping exactly to the pattern. He did wonder if a Stanley knife was the best thing to use for this, but he had got into the way of using it now, and besides, he might never have the chance to use one again. And, placing the pieces on the marked-out paper, he thought it all worked very well.

He let the glue on each piece dry before he went on to the next, because, looking at the angle of the sun, he decided he had made up the lost time that had frightened him earlier. Calm now, he arranged the colours to merge and meld, like the carpet inside on the stairs and the sitting room. From every angle now, as he looked at his work, he thought it was beginning to look like the real thing.

The real thing, however, would need a roof. That could be done. He must not panic again. That would be done as soon as the other things were. He fought down the rising fear, the cold grip on his heart, that the other things would not be ready on time. Time. He had to slow down time. He had to breathe it down. The roof was the thing. He had to tell himself he already possessed what he needed. He had a piece of cardboard from last week's grocery box and – he had done this the night before when he covered the armchairs – it was already covered with red squared paper, sticky for lining shelves. It was a left-over bit, but it worked; and the cardboard that week was thinner than usual, so he would be able to bend it in the middle to make it slant like a proper roof, but it would have to wait till last.

For now, this minute, there was more matchbox work to be done. He stuck eight boxes together, flat on a piece of stiff paper, and was pleased to find that it looked like a bed. He wouldn't paint it or do anything to it, because lots of beds had bluish patterns on their mattresses; and the matchboxes even had a bird on them, a swift, the kind of thing you might find on a bedspread. He set the bed down beside the chairs to dry. The red spider was gone, but a ladybird had come by, a good guardian. He watched her, sitting on his hunkers, conscious now that his throat was dry and his legs tingling, burning with the effort of crouching so long. He should take a break; he should go inside and get his paints. He stretched, catching his breath as he tried to walk on stiffened feet and legs, painful blood rushing through as he started down the path.

It was good to go into the house, cool and, for a moment, nearly too dark to see; his skin felt hot and dry, one forearm turning pink where it had been out of the shade. He let it fall by his side just as Mary turned round from the table, hands and arms and apron dusted with flour. He wasn't quick enough. She drew in a long exasperated breath, wiped one floury hand on her face, and placed her palm on his forehead.

'You're too hot,' she said. 'What were you doing?'

Panic came in quick breaths; he felt his forehead break out in a sweat. What if she came out to see? 'I f-, I fell asleep,' he said, the stammer that had long gone trying to come back. He winced at the lie. He didn't do that. He saw her looking at his arm, and shook it, to show that it worked. 'Bits of me got hot where the bushes didn't come over.' She looked hard at him. He kept his breathing steady; it worked.

'Put your hat on,' she said, turning back to her baking. 'I don't want to be the one to tell your mother you died of sunstroke while she was where she is.'

'Yes, Mary,' he said meekly. 'I mean, no, Mary.'

Half way out the back door he heard her call his name, and stopped, one foot raised. He remembered; he had not collected his paints.

'Yes, Mary?'

'You get to your bed in time tonight. Falling asleep in the morning.'

'I will, Mary. I won't read, even.'

And he turned and walked past her towards the hall and the stairs.

'Where are you off to now?' she asked, head down, clouds of flour rising round her.

'My room,' he said, thinking fast. 'My hat.'

There was no reply. She had forgotten him again. He ran up the stairs, two at a time, the way his father did. There was no noise to get him in trouble, because of the carpet. It really was like his carpet in the garden, and happiness lifted in him to think that he had somehow captured its ... *carpetness*, its *carpetitude*.

He ran down the corridor to the bedroom he shared with John, and it took him just a few minutes to gather together his paints and decide which of the colours would be most suitable. He turned to go. At the door, with only one nervous second's compunction, he went back and lifted a tin of John's as well. It was a magnificent red, like pillar-boxes, and it would be splendid on the front door. It was only a very small tin. They were all small, which was good; he was able to fit every one into the pockets of his shorts, though he clinked a little when he walked. He might have to be Gary Cooper again to get past Mary.

He almost didn't anyway. She collared him as soon as he went into the kitchen, and he thought he was finished; but she just turned him to her and stuck a hat on his head that was not his, probably his father's, smelling of leaves and mould. Through her upraised arms, he saw the pile of baking on the table, its biscuity warmth floating round him. Mary dropped her arms, watched him for a second, then cut and handed him a thick slice of new, warm bread as she pushed him without force towards the back door. 'Get on outside now,' she said. 'Keep that hat on your head. And for goodness sake, stop dreaming.'

The bread was soft and comforting, the fruit in it bitingly hot. The sun warmed him, and the garden waited.

He could just see from the top of the steps his little roofless house waiting under the broom tree. He ran up the path. His carpet with its jewel colours looked bright and strong, the windows and doors miraculously like windows and doors. He wiped his floury hands on his shorts, as he had seen Mary do on her apron. He took a deep breath, sat down on his flattened piece of grass, carefully emptied his pockets, and set them down in the shade. He was completely happy as he set once more to work, painting the armchairs the olive green of aircraft camouflage. It would look like tweed, or leather. Then, while they were drying, he painted the door with John's vibrant red, and for good measure he went round the rims of the windows in the same colour. He was proud that he had so neatly cut out his windows with the Stanley knife.

He lifted out the carpet from its floor, carefully, very carefully, and took out from the bag the pale flowered wrapping paper of an old birthday gift. He brought out the jar of paste he used for his scrapbook, with its special brush. He lifted out the scissors with blunt ends. They had to use those in case they cut themselves; he thought of the Stanley knife, and he smiled to himself a little, as he measured the flowered paper to the walls, and pasted it on with slow care. He smoothed out the bubbles and neatened the edges and corners, his tongue caught between his teeth, so intent that he was surprised after some minutes to feel in his mouth a thin salty trickle, and find that it was blood. He wiped it away, cleaned his hands again on his shorts, and started to replace the carpet, placing the chairs to one side, and the bed to the other. He sat back and looked, and he was pleased. It was a house. It had one floor and one room; perhaps it was a bungalow. Anyway, it was a house.

Almost finished now, he reached into the bag, nearly flat with emptiness, and brought out a package, plastic, fastened at the top with a strip of grey stapled card that caused his teeth to shiver when he touched it. The bag held four little dolls, plastic and tiny enough even for this little house. He reddened, recalling the day he had had to go to the shop on the next road, the everything shop. He had waited outside for nearly half an hour until it was empty, so no one he knew would see him, and he was very glad it wasn't anyone he knew behind the counter; though even the lady serving him had looked oddly at him, a boy in to buy a pack of dolls, but she hadn't said anything; and he was very glad about that too, because if she had, he would have had to leave without buying them, and then the house wouldn't have been right. The house had to have people; but he didn't want to have to go through anything like that ever again. Just thinking about it, he pulled the bag open, almost roughly; but they were so small, the little dolls, and so fragile, that he felt sorry for them, and he lifted them with tender gentleness, placing them with care on the chairs and the bed. And as he looked at them, a sigh that was almost contentment escaped him; he was finally, nearly there.

Then, just as he was reaching into the bag for the red roof, he heard the thud of the car door. His heart jumped against his ribs. They were home. He was not yet ready, but they were home. He didn't know what to do. Thoughts tumbled through his mind; he would be discovered, the surprise would be ruined. Stop, he said to himself. He stopped. He breathed himself calm. He was not going to panic. He had come this far, and there was still a little time. He could leave it all out here until they got settled, because there would be talking and standing round. He heard the baby cry. They would have to settle the baby; that would take time. With all of that going on, nobody would notice him slipping out, and then he could finish it and bring it in and then ...

He forced himself back to the present, and started to clear up, gathering everything he had used and putting it back in the bag. He lifted up any pieces of paper or card he could see lying about. Lastly, he gathered up the Stanley knife and John's almost full tin of red paint and put them carefully in his pocket, because they didn't belong to him. Then, with one final glance behind him, he went down the garden path, running to make it look as if he had been playing. He saw there were traces of red and green paint on his hands, and prayed no one would ask him about that.

The sound of their voices hit him as soon as he opened the back door, so many sounds where there had been silence. The baby, red-faced and overtired, saw him first. She stopped wailing, and held out her arms. He took her from his mother, looked about him, elbowed John, who elbowed him back, and then, there she was. In the centre of the sudden commotion sat his sister, still and quiet, home at last. She was thin as a stick, but she was finally home, and she was going to get better.

This was what he had been waiting for. She would get better; and to help her, he had for her the thing he knew she wanted more than anything in the world. He would tell her now that he had a special surprise for her, and then he would leave her happily guessing while they made her go and lie down, because any minute now they were bound to make her lie down, and then he would go up to the garden and finish everything off. She would never guess what he had made for her, and when it came to the time for bringing it to her, he would see joy on her small pale face. And then he would have his joy.

He handed the baby, happily babbling, over to John and, for once, neither protested. Then quietly, he stepped beside his sister and tapped her on the arm, and she turned round, seeing him for the first time.

'Listen,' he said, 'I've got something to show you, but you've got to ...'

She didn't let him finish.

'No,' she said, pulling herself up by his arm. 'I've got something to show you.'

Haltingly, still holding on, she led him into the sitting room, cool at the front of the house. With her free arm she opened her hand towards the low table. Her other arm squeezed him close.

'Look,' she said. 'Isn't it lovely?'

He could not speak. His mind was whirring and buzzing; he could not think, for on the table stood the most intricate replica of a house that could be imagined. It was pure white, with little windows that looked like diamond panes. It had a smart yellow door, not red, and a porch at one side. The front of the door swung open at the touch of a tiny hook. Inside he saw perfect miniature wooden furniture, table, chairs, fireplace, bath and bed, dressing-table, stove, curtains – even a little clock, a tiny grandfather clock. It had two floors. The knobs on the doors seemed to be of gold, and there were small splendid people, elegantly dressed. On the red tiled roof was a white chimney, with an H-shaped television aerial attached to the top.

'Yes,' he said, eventually. 'It's the very best one I've ever seen.'

FETCH

Eddie, safe under his rock, watched the hailstones bounce off the water. 'Come in out of that,' he heard. Grandma. 'Do you want to catch your death?' Eddie did not want to catch his death; but he wanted to watch the storm pass rippling over the Point and feel the spray of the waves' leap, high over the Churn Rock. But, 'come in,' he heard, 'come in this instant before I go out there and get you!' He scrambled then, back up to the flat ground, with one last turn to look at the grand fury, grey and green below him; and that was when he saw it.

It was as though a chimney or a pipe came out of the water, slowly rising, turning, looking round. Eddie stopped dead. Was it a monster? He was too big – he was ten – he would not believe in monsters, no matter how often they hid beneath the bed and in the press with their guns. He was killed with imagination, they said, before they sent him off to stay at the homeplace with his grandparents.

'You'll like it,' his mother said. 'I did. Indeed, many a time I rue the day I ever left it.'

'You were glad enough to leave,' said his father, 'as I recall.'

He flapped the newspaper and on his face was the look Eddie did not like; but his mother just sighed.

'Many and many's the time,' she said again, and Eddie's heart tightened as he looked at her, teeming the potatoes, hot steam curling the hair that strayed about her face.

Eddie was not sure he wanted to go. He liked his grandparents; he remembered staying with them a long while when he was small, before his father took them to live in the West and he remembered the trust and the safety he had felt; but that was a long time ago. It was too far to visit often now and there was hardly room when they were all there. He liked them, all the same, and he remembered the sound of the sea.

'I'll hear the sea, Mother, won't I?'

'You will, child,' she said, 'day and night, and you'll be safe, please God, out of this.'

She was right. Tucked up in the settle, warm and safe, the wind and the rain savaging round the house, he woke morning after morning to a world washed clean, to bluebells and primroses waving in delight and the sea moving below the house like a living thing. He woke to the sound of his grandmother raking out the range and then he knew his grandfather would soon come down and the day would begin, nothing like the noise and the bustle and the argument of the streets at home.

There was trouble in Dublin. They had been talking about it since last year, since the time they came back from the West. His father wanted to be in the West but his mother did not; she wanted to be with her own people, she said, or nearer them at any rate. The trouble in Dublin was the Rising and sometimes their voices grew angry as they talked of it, in the house and out. In the West, the voices rose and fell into a different rhythm and the language they spoke was soft. In Belfast, the voices were quick and sharp and hard. The Rising was in the newspaper, and Eddie was a good reader. He read about the German war and he knew well that the neighbour men who marched away to the weeping were going to France, and that many of them had not come back and might not ever come back. He knew what a widow was, and he knew plenty of children in school who had no father. He understood that the Rising was another kind of war but he was not allowed to read about it, his mother said, or talk about it either, because it was dangerous, more dangerous than the German war. The talk about it on the streets did not go away, and so Eddie had to, though not the younger ones and the babies, just Eddie; because he was too curious, he heard them say, and he understood too much and he was growing up fast.

The pipe in the water sank down as slowly as it had come up. In a sudden moment Eddie knew what he was seeing, and now he wanted to tell them in the house, because it meant that the German war was nearby. He ran as fast as he could on the uneven tufts but when he got to the house he was not allowed to speak, because he had been too long and he was to sit there and take his good porridge and look out for his Granda coming down while his Grandma, still scolding, went out to see to the hens.

Eddie, alone in the warm kitchen, had no choice but to sit and eat. In spite of himself, the peace and the quiet, the way the hot, smooth porridge with its trace of salt and the milk warm and creamy, slid down inside him, soothed the anxiety. He would tell his Granda the minute he came down and that would be better, because he knew he must not frighten the womenfolk. 'Granda,' he would say, 'I saw a German U-Boat out there in the Lough and it came close by the Churn Rock, close as anything!' And he trusted his Granda would know what to do; maybe he would take the day to think about it, maybe he would say little, but then tell him tonight or tomorrow what was to be done; because if it was the German war coming close there must be something that had to be done. Or maybe it was the Rising? There were guns brought in for that, and they were German too; everybody said so back up in the city. It was one of the things he was not to talk about.

He looked up and there he was, his Granda, on the stairs, coming down in his usual way. Only it was not in his usual way because the stairs did not make their noise, their creaking and cracking that his grandmother said he was to fix when he got a moment. There was no noise now, so he must have got a moment. He came down, and Eddie, unable to wait any longer, started, 'Granda, I saw a ...' but his grandfather neither looked nor stopped, passing silently out the open door. The door slammed shut, as if the wind had caught it. Eddie, big as he was, felt his eyes fill with disappointment.

The door opened. His grandmother came back in, unwinding the shawl from her shoulders.

'Any sign of him yet?' she said, and Eddie looked up, surprised.

'He came down just there, Grandma,' he said. 'Did you not see him?'

'I did not,' she said. 'Do you mean to tell me he went out without a bite?'

Eddie nodded quickly. He did not want her to start being cross with him. 'He just came straight down and went out.'

She made the clucking noise that meant she was displeased. Eddie looked quickly down at his porridge and said no more. She sighed and made to climb the stairs.

'Well, he may go without then, if he's so foolish,' she said. 'A grown man to attempt a day's work on an empty stomach.'

Eddie looked straight at his plate.

'Finish you your breakfast,' she said and as she climbed he heard again the creak of the stairs. His Granda had not finished fixing it then. 'And, mind, come up these stairs when I call you. I want you to help me turn the bed. Come sharp, now – do you hear me, Eddie?'

'Yes, Grandma,' Eddie said and buttered another slice of her warm bread. He would let her cool a little before he went up, in case.

Outside, beyond the small window, the day cleared and settled back into spring. The new leaves on the nearest tree shook away the early rain and a bird sang out from its branches. Eddie wanted to run out into the morning, not go upstairs to turn the heavy mattress, but he knew what he would have to do. Still, rising from the table, he felt his heart lift because the day would not go away, and when his Granda came back he would tell him what he saw. And then he heard his grandmother, but she was not calling him to come.

His heart sank down; he knew that sound. It was the sound he learned in the West, from his own mother when the little baby died and they buried him out there; the only reason she thought of staying away from her own people, not to leave the baby alone. She was *ag caoineadh*, she was making the sound of grief; and something in Eddie froze, and stayed frozen, and though his Grandma called he could not go upstairs. Then she came down slowly and alone, and the stairs creaked with her heavy tread, and her face was grey. And she said would he, like a good boy, go quickly to the next house and get Annie and some of the men, and she was not cross or annoyed in any way but she sank down on the creepy by the fire and she was still there when he came back with Annie and some of the men.

He stood helpless as Annie went straight up the stairs and the men sat down and spoke in low voices; and then Annie called and the men climbed the stairs and Eddie sat down on the settle out of the way until the men brought his Granda down and laid him out in the good room; and his face was greyer than his Grandma's and still. Eddie knew that there he would stay that day and that night and the people would come and go, all of them sorry for his trouble and his grandmother's trouble. He knew that; he had seen all that before and he had heard all the words, except for one. 'The child saw the *fetch*,' he heard them say, looking at him sideways and then looking away. Nobody told him what it meant, but nobody had to tell him.

Outside the bird in the new-leaved tree sang gay and carefree of the bright spring day that no one seemed any longer to see; inside, Eddie, alone on the settle felt his heart sad and heavy. His Granda was dead; he would have to go home to the noise and the danger and he would never, ever get to tell him about the Germans in their underwater boat.

When they came to look for him he did not answer. Tucked under his rock, high above the churning sea, he kept watch, as a man must, for the return of the enemy. He stayed there well into the evening and never went back until he heard his grandmother weeping for him; and he only heard that because the bird had ceased to sing.

THE COCKTAIL HOUR

In Virginia she was a princess, a Southern belle by a
magnolia tree. Even the waiter ignored the others and
made her feel she was a girl again, Daisy Fay before
Gatsby. Mostly she was Scarlett O'Hara, certainly the night
they dined in the hotel whose staircase had been used for
Gone with the Wind. After a day and a half of this he said it
was high time they were going, because he was not
travelling with Scarlett O'Hara another minute. He said he
didn't care how many staircases had been used for *Gone
with the Wind*. He said, in case she had forgotten, there was
work to be done. She said 'why, how you do run on,
Captain Butler.' He said nothing, and they got on the train
for Boston, where her newly-clipped tones gave rise to
terse comment from him.

'Well,' she said, 'you didn't want to travel with a
Southern belle. Right now I'm as played by Katherine
Hepburn.'

'It's something of a relief,' he replied to Harvard Square,
'but, just for me, don't be her all the time.'

Now, increasingly tired, they were on a train to New York. They registered, one to the other, silent recognition when they heard the guard call 'all aboard', just as in films. Past them sped magic names – Mystic, New Haven. They were in a Scott Fitzgerald story, silent, imaginary, through a glass. They said nothing for a long time. Then, quietly, without turning, still looking through the window, he said, 'do you know where I belong?'

She shook her head. It was not clear that he was speaking to her; it was not clear that speech was required.

'I belong in the cocktail hour,' he continued, barely audibly, almost to himself. 'In the Thirties.'

'You're the Thin Man,' she said. 'You're Nick Charles.'

He gazed a long moment at her as if he had just remembered her. He nodded, looking down at his folded hands. Then she said that Nick Charles wasn't really the thin man, that the thin man was the villain whom Nick and Nora caught, after which the name stuck to the series. The words fell into silence, one moment, two.

'Could you,' he said, looking up, 'just leave it there?'

It happened that she had already left it, because she had begun to hear Gershwin, soaring and triumphant inside her head. They were pulling into Penn Station.

'We won't hang round this place,' he said. 'I believe it's dangerous.' They could hear the klaxons of taxicabs; dangerous was exciting too. And now a yellow cab drew up, and from it emerged a jovial, homely black taxi driver who told them his name was Arthur. Arthur and he sat in front after she was handed into the back, by Arthur, who addressed her as 'ma'am.'

'Don't you folks worry none,' said Arthur. 'I'll get you and your wife just anywhere you want to go in this town.'

To this he replied, 'that's not my wife,' and Arthur cast a reproachful look back at her. 'I'm sorry, miss,' said Arthur, and begged her pardon. She thought: Arthur thinks I'm no better than I should be, and the thought made her smile. She looked to see if her companion noted this in the mirror, but his eyes gave no answer. Like a dreamer he gazed at the buildings soaring above them, meeting in the horizon of the sky. He seemed to have forgotten the presence of anyone else in the world. Arthur meanwhile, downcast, kept his eyes on the road in silent dismay. When they pulled up at the hotel Arthur handed her her luggage with his eyes averted. 'Don't forget your mittens, miss,' said his sad old voice, as he gave her her gloves from the back of the seat.

And somewhere between amusement and embarrassment she was still thinking about Arthur as they passed through the opaque glass door of the hotel. When they were in the lobby, they stopped together. They almost collided. Everything looked wrong and smelled wrong. They said nothing, but they exchanged glances as, unusually, he took her elbow, lightly, as if they were crossing a busy road. The lobby was cramped and gloomy, its light garish. Apprehension flowed between them as they walked to the reception desk, where a lazy, unwashed clerk looked them up and down. His badge said: 'Hi. I'm Enrico. How may I help you?' She thought, can this be where they booked us? Yet, even she knew that the Saturday before St Patrick's they would get nowhere else.

'You're lucky we kept these rooms,' said the clerk. 'You're not early, and it's Saturday night.'

'Enrico,' he said. His voice was level, but his hands on the edge of the desk were whitening. 'We've been on a train for six hours. We can't help the time of our arrival.'

The clerk shrugged and said, 'I don't make the rules.'

There was a long silence. She looked up at her companion, and noted, irrelevantly, that he was a surprisingly tall man. He is not heavy, she thought, but he is tall. Nor, at that moment, could she read the expression on his face. All she felt was the edge of fear.

'We'll take a look at the rooms,' he said, spreading his hands wide on the desk, 'before we decide whether we stay or not.'

He leaned slightly forward, and she noticed the hands beginning to form themselves into fists. The fear edged further in.

'Suit yourself,' said the clerk, with a shrug, 'but you're booked in advance, and I'll have to charge you anyway.'

The two men, one small and lithe, the other long and poised, looked hard at one another. The clerk's face was insolent, amused; her companion's, as he turned away suddenly, a shuttered mask.

Enrico did not make a move to help them with their bags. Neither did the heavy, silent porter slumped in a swivel chair, watching him so far with detachment, watching her with something else. She saw this, and picking up her bags with as defiant a gesture as their weight would permit, moved to the lift clanking slowly, endlessly, to the ground. She thought fleetingly of Mary Astor, face shadowed by the crossed bars of the lift, led down to her execution, Bogart watching, his face impassive but for the haunted eyes and the sardonic mouth.

This lift reeked of alcohol and other, worse things. Hospital, she thought. Urine and vomit and sickness. They were silent. She could hear her heart and thought she could hear his. His upper lip was slightly lifted, as if in distaste. The lift was slow and creakingly noisy, the odour foul. He was white, almost blue round the mouth. For a moment she was sure he would pass out in the rancid, cramped space. Then, as it seemed they could endure not one second longer, they thudded to a lurching stop. Beyond the bars they could see and smell dank walls and mouldy carpets. He took in a long breath, and holding the lift doors open with one foot as he hefted the luggage out, said, 'let's get you to yours first. Then I'll look at mine.'

He left her bags just inside her room. This was hard, because the heavy door was narrow and geared to automatic, immediate closure. He was breathing hard.

'I'll be back in a minute,' he said. 'I want you to bar this door and not open it to anyone but me. Do you hear?'

She nodded and, turning in some trepidation, switched on the light. It flickered, clicked, flicked, wavered and finally flashed into white, pitiless light and she saw grimy net curtains above a corroded, flaking radiator; a lopsided, nylon-covered bed with greying sheets. Looking in the bathroom, carefully touching nothing, she sensed before seeing that the lavatory had not been flushed. On the dark-ringed bath, a small square of scum-covered soap half-lay in a paper wrapper. A used condom, torn, was placed upon the still-dripping shower head. She thought, rent apart, rent by the hour.

The door was knocked. Three sharp raps. Two short raps. She let him in, almost taking him by the hand. His face was terrible, a Mount Rushmore head. He was utterly white, as if he had been sick in the interim. He looked round the room, and shaking his head, like a swimmer shaking water, moved slowly past her. He leaned against the lintel of the dirty bathroom. His back was bent, his shoulders stooped. Though the room was chilly, even cold, she saw him wipe perspiration from his face with a handkerchief. He tapped his teeth with the forefinger of a clenched fist.

'Mine smells even worse,' he said, and sat down on the filthy bed as if his legs had suddenly given way. He looked so ill that she stopped herself from telling him that she thought the sheets might be alive. He lifted the phone.

'Whatever about me,' he said, as though to himself, 'I can't have you stay in a place like this.'

In that second her astonished heart took flight, not to Virginia, not to the magnolia tree, but to a place immeasurably beyond, a soaring sky that was now and forever, while the filthy, sordid room fell away like the sea below the eagle. From that light and dizzy place she watched as he replaced the receiver, and put his head in his hands.

'We're not connected,' he said. She thought, what does he mean? How can we not be connected? His voice was low, despairing. 'He won't connect us until he knows we're staying.'

Now giddy with understanding she waved her hand. 'Oh, he's charging us anyway. Tell him we're staying. Tell him anything.'

He lifted his hands from his head and something that was almost a smile began about his mouth. He said, 'is that Miss Hepburn talking, or Miss Scarlett?'

'It's just me,' she said, 'just me.'

Still looking at her he put his hand on the telephone. And sitting in the suddenly magical room she wondered without anything more than mild surprise how it was that she had never noticed he had the face of an angel. Quite unable to look, she turned away and, as from a great distance, heard him speak into the phone, but did not hear any of what he said. Her heart was too much filled. There was no more fear. The room was music; it was light.

Then gradually, slowly, she floated down from the place where she had been and remembered that they were in a fearful situation, that the room was filthy and foul. She noticed, as one who wakes from a dream, that he had stopped speaking. She heard rather than saw him writing, scratching something with a stubby pencil on a dirty piece of paper beside the bed. He handed this to her.

The tension broke. She laughed. 'Your writing,' she said. 'It's appalling. This looks like Death Club to me. You've booked us into a place called the Death Club?'

He reached across, and taking it from her, gently, silently, put it in his pocket. He said, 'we are going to a place called the Downtown Athletic Club.'

'Which is?'

He said, 'an athletic club, I think.'

He reached out his hand and raised her to her feet. 'I understand it's downtown.' And, without any further words, they pushed open together the unyielding door.

She did not notice the smells in the lift going down. She did not care that they were charged for rooms they did not use. She scarcely paused to notice the language of the boys in the gauntlet they ran from the door to the kerb to dive into the yellow cab. She felt slightly drunk.

Safely in the cab, he gave the address, and leaned back beside her on the leather seat. She could feel him breathing. Their heads were almost touching. She could smell his aftershave, expensive, subtle and mixed with it fresh perspiration, not unpleasant, quite the reverse, like that from an athlete. The Downtown Athletic Club. Now she heard her own breathing. Just in that moment, they were completely relaxed, entirely at ease.

And then, without warning, he leaned closer, and very quietly, almost like a lover, began to speak.

'Here's a story for you,' he said. 'You write it. Maybe it's a movie. Two people get off a train. They've been travelling for many days in a strange and wonderful country. They're tired. They're dizzy and dazzled, and they don't even know what period they're in. They hardly know who they are. They have quite a bit of luggage. One of them has many books. The other one is carrying them. He has a red mark on his shoulder from carrying them, but he carries them willingly. They are in a taxi, going to an address. They have been very badly frightened, and the address sounds good to them. It sounds like heaven, like home. But they don't really know where it is, because they've never been to New York before.'

They were parked at lights. Stop. Go. Don't walk. Don't even think about parking here. His voice dropping almost to a whisper he continued, 'and where did they get this address? From an anonymous voice on a phone in a sleazy room. Why should they trust this voice? Maybe they're being set up. Maybe not. Maybe this happens all the time – maybe there is a ring, a group who send unsuspecting tourists to lonely places and murder them. How do they know?'

'Then, suppose they arrive, and to their relief feel the taxi stop in, let's say, the financial area of town. That's solid, isn't it? The financial area? Wall Street? The air is cold. They can smell the sea. They are right down at the tip of the island, at the Battery.'

She interrupted, 'the Park is up and the Battery's down,' but he continued, quite as though she had not uttered. His voice was dreamy, mesmeric, 'there is a large building covered in scaffolding and plastic. They get out of the taxi, so relieved to have arrived, and wait for the driver to help them with their luggage from the boot. But he doesn't. No sooner are they outside than he drives away. Nothing but tail lights and the screech of brakes. Then nothing. Silence. They are alone in the darkness of the New York night with no luggage. It is deathly quiet. Nothing much happens in the financial area at night. Nothing at all, in fact. And then in the silence, the eerie nothing silence, they see a door opening, a slow door, a widening square of light in the scaffolding. Out come one, two, five, seven big guys. All young. Big. Young guys. Black maybe. Maybe Hispanic. Like those guys who taunted us outside the hotel. You remember?'

She nodded. She remembered.

'Maybe they're even the same ones. Maybe they took their own taxi. They are holding – no, brandishing – bits of hosepipe and rubber piping and chains. One of them, bigger than the rest, very good-looking, very threatening, with even white teeth, smiles at the two people on the kerb, wrapping a heavy chain round his big, powerful hand. And he says, 'welcome to the Downtown Athletic Club.'

Lights again. Stop. Go. Red flashing. Green. She thought, could we get out? Could we run? She looked across at him. He had leaned away from her once more, head slumped upon his chest. His bones were very sharp. In that second, he looked like the prisoners who survived, or did not survive, Auschwitz. She thought, he means it, this will happen.

And sure enough, the air grew colder. They were down by the sea, and she thought, we are going down to the end of the island; we are at the edge of the world and no one knows.

Then, with a lurch, the taxi swerved across the road.

'Here you are, folks,' said the taxi driver, in a voice surprisingly normal. They looked at each other. Out of the window they could see scaffolding and green plastic. Her heart began to pound again, but in a low, feeble fashion, like a heart that has died twice and cannot make the effort another time. He inclined once more toward her, as if to speak. She thought of the Kennedy assassination, Jackie's memory of her husband turning, slumping toward her with his hand to his throat. Jackie said later she had only one thought, 'his mouth is so neat.' It was like that moment, but he was not shot. He was not slumping. It was just a moment, and the story could be changed if they could do the right thing. She felt between them a final, despairing resolve to rise to the occasion and to do what had to be done, together, now. His mouth was so neat.

And then, as suddenly as it had come, the moment passed. They stepped out of the cab, and standing on the kerb, in the quiet street they had so vividly foreseen, the dark dream somehow dissipated. The quiet street was only quiet. And the driver, sweet and normal as Arthur, did not speed off but helped them in quiet courtesy with their bags and accepted their modest tip with some graciousness. They turned, in near astonishment, to the door. And they saw it open, slowly, felt themselves bathed in light, and saw a tall, elegantly-uniformed doorman come easily down the steps, reaching for the bags, frozen in their hands. He said, 'welcome to the Downtown Athletic Club.'

Through a door of glass, they stepped into the thirties, to the home of the Heisman trophy, to an entrance hall as big as a ballroom, to heavy gleaming furniture and soft lights, to a place that was waiting for them. Momentarily, she closed her eyes. When she opened them it was all still there. Suddenly weak, she leaned against the edge of one of the deep sofas and said, 'have we arrived?' He said, 'we have. And just in time for cocktails.'

And looking at him she saw, not a tired colleague in crumpled travelling clothes, but a handsome, austere man in a dinner jacket, a man with style and flair and panache, with just a little, a delicious hint of the reckless, the dangerous. She saw Nick Charles. And in that instant, she was his haughty, sophisticated Nora, somewhere in the thirties, one pencilled eyebrow quizzically raised, a slender cigarette holder in her fingers, a single witty bracelet on her wrist.

For the second time that evening, he took her arm. And finally, utterly themselves, they drifted into their club, an elegant pair, looking for the cocktail lounge.

CRITICAL RESPONSES TO THE AUTHOR'S WORK

– *May Lou and Cass: Jane Austen's Nieces in Ireland* (Blackstaff, 2011)

'An intriguing story, and so invitingly told.'

– Hermione Lee

'The book I enjoyed most this year ... elegant, very intelligent and witty, like Jane Austen herself.'

– Medbh McGuckian (*Belfast Telegraph*, December 2011)

– *The Friday Tree* (Ward River Press/Poolbeg 2014)

'Your writing is an absolute beauty. Brigid and Francis ... will captivate the readers – and will certainly also grip them as they gripped me. And what then made me tingle was the chapter "George".'

– David Marcus

'A vivid and intimate portrayal of childhood's confused stumbling into the complex tragedies of the adult world.'

– David Park

'Exquisite ... Because the reader is at all times aware of the horrors that lie ahead, the narrative charm of this delightful novel has an added depth.'

– Eugene McCabe

'An engrossing story, elegantly told ... a lovely prose style, crisp and flowing, and imbued with warmth and real humanity.'

– Donal Ryan

'This brand-new novel reads already like a classic.'

– Anthony Glavin, *Sunday Times*, 30 March 2014

– *The Way We Danced* (Ward River Press/Poolbeg 2016)

'I never read novels ... but I found this one captivating, enchanting, delicious, even sumptuous.'

– Medbh McGuckian

'Vivid and compelling.'

– Patricia Craig, *Irish Times*, 24 December 2016

© Bobbie Hanvey Photographic Archives, Boston College

Sophia Hillan began her writing career with prizes for her first short stories from the BBC (1979) and Listowel Writers' Week (1980), publication in 'New Irish Writing' (*Irish Press*) and a shortlisted nomination for a Hennessy Award (1981). She went on, while pursuing a parallel academic life, first as Fellow (1986–1988), then Assistant Director of Queen's University Belfast's Institute of Irish Studies (1993–2003), to be shortlisted for the Royal Society of Literature's first V.S. Pritchett Memorial Award (1999), to be published in David Marcus's first *Faber Book of Best New Irish Short Stories* (2005) and to have her work commissioned and broadcast by BBC Radio 4. She published her Ph.D on Michael McLaverty as *In Quiet Places* (1989) and *The Silken Twine* (1992) and, after uncovering the previously untold story of Jane Austen's Donegal connection, went on to publish her research as *May, Lou and Cass: Jane Austen's Nieces in Ireland* (2011). She has since published two novels, *The Friday Tree* (2014) and *The Way We Danced* (2016). Her work has most recently been published in Alan Hayes' *Reading the Future: New Writing from Ireland* (2018). *The Cocktail Hour* is her first short story collection.